Jean Middlemas

Sackcloth and Broadcloth

Vol. I

Jean Middlemas

Sackcloth and Broadcloth
Vol. I

ISBN/EAN: 9783337049546

Printed in Europe, USA, Canada, Australia, Japan

Cover: Foto ©Andreas Hilbeck / pixelio.de

More available books at **www.hansebooks.com**

SACKCLOTH AND BROADCLOTH.

A NOVEL.

BY

JEAN MIDDLEMASS,

AUTHOR OF ' WILD GEORGIE,' ' SEALED BY A KISS,' ' INNOCENCE AT PLAY,' ETC., ETC.

IN THREE VOLUMES.

VOL. I.

TINSLEY BROTHERS,
CATHERINE STREET, STRAND,
LONDON.
1881.

SACKCLOTH AND BROADCLOTH.

CHAPTER I.

GUIDE, PHILOSOPHER, AND FRIEND.

"QUID brevi fortes jaculamus ævo Multa," if one may be allowed the seeming incongruity of quoting Horace to a lady,' and the Rev. Lawrence Sivewright lounged luxuriously in his chair as though thorough enjoyment was the *ne plus ultra* of life.

'My dear father had me initiated in a little Latin. I suppose you mean that more work would exhaust your vitality and deepen, before middle age, the furrows on your brow?' said Mrs Desborough in a soft voice, pointing her words with just that happy admixture of compliment and sneer, of which only a woman knows the proportions.

The vicar laughed—for he was the vicar of the parish, this elegant disciple of Epicurus —and he was quite fifty, notwithstanding Mrs Desborough's kindly allusion to the date when he should reach the usually long halting place between youth and old age.

'Only dry wood burns steadily,' he answered, using metaphor, a mode of speech in which he frequently indulged. 'Why introduce damp twigs which are the mere offshoots of young half-grown trees, unless for the sake of squandering your energies by the perpetual use of the bellows?' Mrs Desborough shrugged her shoulders; but before we follow their conversation sufficiently to reach its subject-matter, a sketch in black and white of place and people were perhaps convenient.

Vantage Park is a grand old seignorial estate, situated in a northern county about twelve miles from the sea. An architectural digression, long enough to form a volume in itself, might be made out of its gables, architraves, corbels, mullions and gargoyles, not to allude to more than one stirring epoch of which those ancient walls have been mute witnesses in times gone by. But in the year of grace 1869, the possessors of Vantage Park, endowed to the fullest with this world's goods, had made it the abode of luxury and modern art. True, the squire loved the traditions of his race and name, and secretly revered the old pile for its time-honoured descent ; nay, it is even whispered that he made a daily pilgrimage to a particular column, whereon was faintly inscribed a date that conveyed a twelfth-century recollection to his mind. But of the cheery pleasant-tempered artistic little squire anon. ' He is but a cipher in the great account.'

Mrs Desborough holds the reins, and governs house and lands.

Sitting gracefully on a satin sofa, knitting usefully for the poor, and talking, oh! so softly and complacently to the vicar, Mrs Desborough, with her calm white countenance, matronly figure undulating with creamy lace, and her genial smile, scarcely looks a formidable dame. Still, given the velvet exterior which charms and holds a fresh acquaintance captive, her eyes—mark! we did not speak of eyes in the pleasant picture—they are usually half shut, under drooping lids, but seldom are they allowed to tell the latent thought ; besides, although you scarcely own it even to yourself, there is a barricade of manner between you and Mrs Desborough. It arises probably from a consciousness of her own superiority, which she cannot help displaying—unwillingly it is true, for Mrs Desborough spreads her net to please, though she is the mother of two grown-up sons. She likes what she calls the intellectual companionship of men—perhaps she does not altogether stop there—and craves something more than mental flattery in her relations with the sterner sex; but, alas! Mrs Desborough was born a *precieuse*, and in displaying too freely her blue stockings, well-shaped though the feet and ankles are they encase, she loses the power of mere womanliness.

History, chronology, especially as to the births, deaths, and marriages of her acquaintances, linked with an unconquerable predilection for the Dutch school of word painting, are characteristics, taken collectively, which must nip in the bud as a keen March wind, any utterances of tenderness. What so freezing as a tedious detail—a long episode of the reign of Phillipe le Bel, carefully elaborated, or more annihilating than a wordy lecture on the absolute necessity of being useful to your fellows? No, Mrs Desborough in her efforts to be admired, lost the chance of being loved.

Yet the Rev. Lawrence Sivewright, vicar

of Fernwood-cum-Grasdale, a fat living in
the gift of the owner of Vantage Park, was
on terms of close intimacy with the lady of
the house. It was an alliance based on the
usual premises, antithetical opinions; hence
argument was the pumice stone which pre-
vented rust from corroding their friendship.

Vantage Park, with its ever hospitable
reception, was a pleasant lounge for the
vicar, who appreciated fully the comfortable
appointments of the establishment, the
luscious wines of which the cellar boasted,
and above all what he was wont to call
the 'ambrosia,' provided by M. Baptiste,
who was a veritable cordon bleu. Not
that Mr Sivewright's bachelor surroundings
were very inferior in luxury to those of the
great house, for this modern Lucullus, with
his classical proclivities and self-indul-
gent—we had almost written sensual—
habits, had metamorphosed the vicarage into
an abode of luxury which more resembled

a villa of old Tusculum than the working quarters of a plain steady-going English clergyman. Mr Sivewright's appearance was in strict accordance with his tastes. He was tall, in his youth had probably been slight; but now his *embonpoint* almost amounted to obesity, though it could never degenerate into coarseness, for seldom does high breeding stand in such good stead as when age or indulgence have banished the more transitory attributes of humanity. Mr Sivewright had a noble head, a calm philosophic brow; his hair, which was iron grey, grew plentifully, and just turned into a curl, perhaps naturally; it were scarcely seemly in so dignified a personage to hint at art; yet only valets know the trifles by which great triumphs are completed. His face was closely shaven, the dark well-formed eyebrows, and the clear speaking eyes were its chief beauties. The nose was Roman, and well-nigh perfect in shape, yet the possibility of an ideal man vanished as you looked at the full ruddy lips with their epicurean expression.

Dress manifestly was one of Mr Sivewright's especial studies, and not only was he never seen with a speck or flaw on his broadcloth, but the form and texture were to him matters of interest ; nor did he rigidly, except on state occasions, adhere to the ordained churchman's garb, as did his neighbour and dear brother in orders, the Rev. Mr Lently, even to exaggeration, almost amounting to caricature.

As Mr Sivewright sits now in Mrs Desborough's morning-room, quoting Horace in that clear, well-educated voice of his which, together with his elegant scholarship, might with more energy have made him an orator, he feels that the ground on which he rests is trembling as if by electricity—he is sensible of disruptive signs—an earthquake is at hand. His long white fingers paddle among his silvered locks, and he mentally observes that there has been an interview between Mrs Desborough and his reverend brother Lently, whom he ever designates as the disturber of peace. It is against Mr Sivewright's creed to give way to strong language and vituperative epithets. Yet Ritualism is his *bête noire*, he endures it with a smile and denounces it more in acts than words, though never perhaps does he feel more inclined to throw off his apathy and fight for his rights, than when the Rev. Luke Lently, the ritualistic thunderer of the adjacent parish, makes a descent on Vantage Park and seeks to convert the lady of the house to his peculiarly limited views.

Mrs Desborough is angry. She shrugs her shoulders and knits very fast; but, like her classical friend, she has her feelings under command, and for a moment or two she does not speak.

'What does he mean by damp twigs and bellows? If any one ever wanted rousing he does himself. It is the old story of the mote and the beam.' At last she breaks out, darting with woman's love of sudden digression into another branch of the subject. 'It is not that I hold all Mr Lently's views, though I think there is much good in some of them ; but I do wish I could see a little new work begun in this parish.'

'Heaven forbid !' fervently ejaculated the vicar.

'My dear Mr Sivewright, you need not disturb yourself. I shall be only too happy to qualify for a machine. Giving the people objects of interest and usefulness would help to smooth away some of the difficulties of one's own life.'

And she sighed as though the last part of the sentence was pregnant with meaning. The vicar declined the hidden interpretation by a straightforward answer.

'Increase them tenfold, you mean, my dear friend, by setting an immense amount of parochial machinery in motion which you will be powerless to stop. All these innovations are, as you know, quite against my conservative views. Let us keep the people as they were primitively, "hewers of wood and drawers of water!" These so-called reforms only defeat their own ends, and render the *profanum vulgus* totally unfit for duty. Progression applied to the lower orders is the crying mistake of the century; feed them, clothe them if you like, but—'

'Really, Mr Sivewright, this is going too far. Has not every healthy child that is born a heart and head as well as a stomach? What did Heaven make them for?'

'Use naturally; but not use artificially. If you turn a common field flower into an exotic, it is no longer a field flower. It becomes a specimen of a totally different plant, unless, indeed, it dies in the forcing. Since Providence has instituted diversity, why should we attempt to establish oneness by lowering

ourselves to the level of the masses, which
we must necessarily do in our endeavours
to raise them to our standard.   Against all
this abominable democracy nature rebels.'

' But they have souls to save ! '

Mr Sivewright bowed his head and looked
at his filbert nails.

' They worship Heaven in the fulness of its
power, its works, its benefits—in fact, what
more do you want ? '

' But Mr Lently says—'

A smile spread itself over Mr Sivewright's
countenance; he looked radiant when most
men would have been angry.

' With your erudition, your broad free
views, your capability for grasping the truth,
I am surprised that you should do more than
feel amused by the study of Lently's " Guide
to Heaven."   Poor fellow ? '

' Mr Lently is very zealous, he can scarcely
fail to reach the desired goal, while we—Mr
Sivewright, I am beset by many scruples.'

'Since this morning. Mr Lently lunched here, I fancy?'

'You do not object to my indulging occasionally in a little conversation with those who do not altogether think as you do?' asked the lady very humbly.

'Certainly not, my dear Mrs Desborough, certainly not. "Truth loves open dealing." If you or any of my parishioners feel that you are made happier by following the road of which Mr Lently has installed himself as signpost, pray do not let me be considered for a moment in the matter. My desire is that every one should discover what he or she feels to be the truth. All minds are not constituted alike—to some it is veiled in spiritual types, to some it is clear and unhidden.'

'Ah!' said Mrs Desborough, as though her thoughts were beyond expression in words, and she laid her knitting in her lap, and folded her hands over it.

Mr Sivewright's was pleasant, gentleman-

like, easy teaching. She would follow it
gladly, if only that Mr Lently would not cross
her path, and by uprooting all her calcula-
tions, fill the air with scruples, and bring
about those occasional small earthquakes
which dislodged, for a time at least, all the
placidity and geniality of the social relations
of life.

'Then there is Matthew,' she observed
after a short pause. It seemed a somewhat
illogical remark, but to the initiated it had its
sequence, as Mr Sivewright's answer proved.

'Matthew is passing through the unstable
period of extreme youth—his principles are
by no means fixed. You surely would not
allow him to influence you ?'

'Yet he is going to take orders.'

'Just so—in time. Before that time
arrives there may be many changes.'

'Really, Mr Sivewright, you are not encouraging to-day; and from such a friend as
you are, I always look for help.'

' Yet you sip the waters of every fountain, and imagine each one a Hippocrene.'

' Pardon me, when poetry and the arts are in question, I never desert you ; but you are scarcely the Delphic oracle—is it not a voice rather than a mere human friend one wants to reveal the secrets of mystic life ? '

' Thereon hangs the whole question of a priesthood.'

And Mr Sivewright rose as though the priestly dignity were one which his shoulders, developed though they were—yet scarcely felt broad enough to carry.

The interruption was timely, for the sound of voices in the hall told of an arrival, and in another moment Mrs Desborough was in the arms of her eldest son, who for some months had been abroad seeing a little life on his own account—a good deal more than was good for him, if the truth were told.

' My darling George !' and she looked into his face and smoothed the hair off his

brow, as though she would still find the
baby among his features, for George was
Mrs Desborough's favourite child, 'the
glory and the darling of the old manorial hall.'

'You look charming, mother. How are
the rest? Is Matt going to take orders,
young noodle? I beg your pardon, Mr
Sivewright, but you know you are an exception. I always forget you are a parson.
I have got lots to tell you. You'll ask me
to dinner some night at the vicarage; won't
you?'

'Yes, my dear young friend, whenever you
like, so long as you bring a contribution to
the feast in the form of anecdote.'

'Ay will I, and good stories too.'

And they shook hands warmly, for the
vicar would have accused himself of want
of tact if he had intruded farther on the
tête-à-tête, in which he believed, and truly,
that mother and son would gladly indulge
after a long separation.

CHAPTER II.

TABLE TALK.

'ON a l'age de son coeur,' they say. This being so, Mrs Desborough was on the sunny side of thirty, whereas, in reality, she had completed her fifth decade ; but impressionable natures are apt to maintain perpetual youth, and Mrs Desborough was very sensible to impressions. Her character presented a curious mixture of cleverness and weakness ; in fact, she might have been in danger of passing for rather a silly woman, but for her rare educational advantages ; consequently her mind ran riot on theories instead of trifles. She was more or less under the mental dominion of the Rev. Lawrence Sivewright, though, for the sake of argument, she usually fought his opinions at every issue.

To-day, however, Mr Lently has had his turn, and been listened to with a degree of interest which has made him almost believe in the conversion of the mistress of Vantage Park ; but already a counter power has sprung up in the person of her son George, than whom Mr Sivewright could not have a more able coadjutor. The dinner-bell has just been rung, and Mrs Desborough sails in her soft quiet way into the room to join the family party there assembled before dinner. The squire and his son are talking on the hearthrug.

' The dinner-bell has rung ages. Whom are we waiting for ?' asked George, after some minutes had been passed in farther conversation with the squire, his mother meanwhile looking out of the window.

' For Matthew, I suppose ?'

'Matthew? Since when has he become a defaulter in hours? Where is he? We surely are not going to wait for him?' and this time George addresses his father.

'Mr Matthew has not come in yet,' at this moment announces the butler, 'and dinner is served.'

Matthew Desborough was like his mother, precise in matters of detail, vague and shifty in opinions, while he possessed even more than her natural amount of cleverness. His present absence was then the more remarkable, in that it was unusual. If George had been late or not forthcoming at dinner time, no one would have observed it; but with Matthew the case was different, and each of the family formed his or her own conclusions as to the cause as they went in to dinner.

Matthew, during a long and highly dangerous illness, had been converted to Mr Lently's tone of thought, but had scarcely sufficiently cultivated among other Christian virtues that of tolerance; perhaps because he felt that by giving way to invective against others he was rendering his own ground more secure. Be it as it might, he railed smartly against what he deemed his brother's heathenism, and suffered cruelly, in that his words seldom called forth more than a smile from either George or Mr Sivewright, who were nearly allied in their contempt for, rather than their dread of, Matthew's and Mr Lently's school.

The dinner, with its many courses, dawdled on, interspersed with such fragmentary conversation as the presence of the servants permitted, during which let us finish our portrait-painting with sketches of father and son.

Mr Desborough was a little fussy good-tempered garrulous man, his small talk being amusing, because generally on artistic subjects, and rendering him more or less a favourite with every one excepting his wife, who did not deny the fact that the squire's tongue, like the dripping of perpetual water, became monotonous, and bored her. He was a thorough little gentleman—we might almost say courtier—and it would have galled Mrs Desborough not a little had she known that many of the invitations they received were more for the pleasure of enjoying his cheery society than for the sake of her prosy detailed stories.

George, their eldest son, scarcely resembled either of his parents, except that he was thoroughly well-bred—a birthright of which a very free indulgence in the fashionable slang and fast manners of the day had not succeeded in depriving him. He was tall, good-looking, with a genial happy face; owing to an amount of inborn philosophy the troubles and disappointments of life affected him but little.

' If you can't get the thing you want

the most, take the next best and be happy,'
was the motto of George Desborough's life ;
and he was one of the very few who
succeed in leading a don't-care existence
gracefully.

Dinner has come to an end, and still
Matthew is an absentee. Mrs Desborough
is a little anxious ; a violent storm that
had raged in the afternoon makes her fear
she knows not what. A footstep is heard
crossing the hall ; the important-looking
butler comes once more into the room.

' Mr Matthew ? ' she asks, showing her
family for the first time where her thoughts
have been straying during dinner.

No ; the servants' entrance has naught to
do with Matthew. It is a note from the
Duchess of Montarlis, conveying an invitation
to Montarlis Castle for the following week.
A curious little fluster manifests itself in the
manner of the mistress of Vantage Park,
during which Matthew is entirely forgotten

and Mr Lently's lecture on the vanities of life are conspicuously absent from the lady's mind.

In the weakness of her human nature Mrs Desborough—established though her own position is—is not, with all her cleverness and sense of self-superiority, above having her vanity tickled and her pulse quickened each time she is brought into intimate relations with the very great lady of the county — her dear friend, the Duchess of Montarlis.

'A dinner or what?' inquires George. 'I hate a ragamuffin *fête* when the duke asks all the voting lot.'

'You are not invited, George; but then of course the dear duchess does not know you have returned. It is a dinner this time—on the 24th. The invitation is only for your father and me. Shall I accept, Richard?'

'Yes, dear, if you like, of course. We have no other engagement I presume. I

wonder who will be there ? Not the Lancelot
Cairns I hope. I took that mummy-headed
woman into dinner the last time, and she is
a bore. Oh! Sivewright; he is sure to be
asked. We can offer to drive Sivewright
over if he is going.'

'The duchess never gives a party without
Mr Sivewright; of that you may be very
sure.' And there was a strong emphasis on
the never. George set up a shout of laughter,
at which he received a look from his mother,
which spoke a volume of rebuke, but he paid
no attention, only went on laughing, and
asked ironically,—

'Do you think exalted rank makes people
stricter, mother mine ?'

'I don't know what you mean, George
The dear duchess has very religious tendencies, and the duke is quite evangelical.'

'So I should suppose. He would not
stand Lently at any price.'

'No; although they are not in his parish,

I think Mr Sivewright directs the family
consciences. The duchess—'

'Now, mother, be accurate; you are
generally so scrupulous in matters of detail.'

'Well, they do say,' and Mrs Desborough
prepared for a story in true narrative form,
while George heaped his plate with fruit,
for though he quite believed his mother
would discover a good point at last, he imagined she would be tolerably prolix before
she got there. 'You have not heard, my
dear George,' she went on, 'how should
you, since you have been away—the little
tale about Mr Sivewright and the duchess?
I believe it is quite true, though Mr Sivewright only laughs whenever I vaguely allude
to it. It seems then that the duchess (it was
before Mr Lently came) was beset by religious scruples. She had spent some months
in Italy—what happened there who shall
say? but her head had been filled with
ideas about auricular confession, at which

the duke was quite aghast.   Well, one morning, soon after her return home, she drove
over in her pony carriage to Fernwood
Vicarage, and asked for a private interview
with the vicar.'

For a second or two George held a
plum hesitatingly between his mouth and
his plate, and then put it down before
him and gave his undivided attention to
the riper fruit his mother offered him.

'What passed has not been exactly di-
vulged,' went on Mrs Desborough.   'Only
a few days afterwards the duke sent for Mr
Sivewright in order to speak with him
anent something important.   On his arrival
at Montarlis Castle he found the duke—
you know he can look very fierce when he
likes—perfectly livid with anger.   But who
so great an adept at pouring balm on open
wounds as our facile vicar?   He succeeded
not only in pacifying, but in reassuring the
duke.'

'Well, go on. You are not going to leave a fellow there. What happened?'

'The duke's evangelical bristles were up; in fact he did not altogether understand the sort of creed Mr Sivewright professed. From hearing him preach the Sunday before, he came to the somewhat rash conclusion that the divine's unction had *entrain*, that he gave evidence of a fresh accession of religious life. With a confusion of ideas for which you know the dear duke is proverbial, he also settled it in his mind that Mr Sivewright's sanctity must be inseparable from what he calls the new-fangled church views which are creeping into the country. He therefore summoned the vicar in order to make him promise, as a man of honour, that nothing should induce him to hear the duchess's confession, however much pressed.'

'Sivewright, surpliced, shriving the duchess, what a caricature it would make! Why the deuce did she not go to Lently? But go on, finish the story. What did Sivewright say ?'

'It was before Mr Lently came. Our vicar met his grace's tirade with a smile of mingled pity and amusement, and having contemplated him with his head on one side for full a minute and a half, merely said, in that velvety voice of his we all know so well, " My dear duke, I hope to keep my reputation of being a respectable member of society, but before I shrive yours or any man's wife —Heaven forgive me !—I'll kiss her." '

'No !' and George roared with laughing till the room rang again, ' No, that is the man in a sentence. He merits immense κυδος. Kiss the duchess ! and he actually said that to the duke ?'

'Who was so relieved by the discovery that they have been firm friends ever since ; but Mr Sivewright is very clever you know.' And Mrs Desborough gave a little sigh.

'It is all an invention, Minnie, a horrid

country side fabrication. I can't think how you can circulate it. George, pass the wine.'

Still the squire looked amused. He scarcely wished it not to be true.

' I'll ask Sivewright about it the first time I am with him alone,' put in George. ' Kiss the duchess! Well she is tempting enough. Do you think the duke would let me try ?'

' My dear George! you don't imagine for a moment that Mr Sivewright really did mean to kiss her ; he is far too correct. It is only a little playful way he has of strengthening his words by a practical allusion ; and Mrs Desborough looked the very incarnation of prudery, which only, however, called forth another fit of tempestuous hilarity from her son.

' The dear credulous mother! she believes in the sanctity of every sinner— even in mine, I do think.'

' I don't know about you, but I feel quite

sure about Mr Sivewright,' she said, rising and going towards the door.

George sprang up to open it for her, giving her a hearty kiss as she passed him.

During the temporary amusement Matthew had been forgotten, but he put himself in evidence at that moment by appearing suddenly at the other end of the hall. 'Why, George, when did you come?' he called out as he saw his brother.

'And you, you truant, where have you been?'

Yes, where had Matthew been? There was a flush on his cheeks and a light in his eyes, which even Mrs Desborough failed to read, anxiously and inquiringly though she looked at him.

CHAPTER III.

LOVE'S YOUNG DREAM.

IT is an oppressively warm, almost sultry afternoon. Storm clouds veil the sun, and all nature seems lazy, inert, and at rest. The very insects have ceased their buzzing and their gambols, the birds their twittering and their flight. Shelter from the coming rain is the instinctive craving of all living creation, excepting evidently the human, for a girl is wandering slowly through a little copse which 'skirts the road, as fringe upon a petticoat.' She seems totally regardless of the large rain drops which are already pattering among the leaves above her head.

Perhaps she delights in storm and wind
and wet; yet she is scarcely a girl of a
daring type—there is neither fire nor determination in her countenance; she is simply
a modest-looking Saxon maiden on whom
the good fairy who presided at her birth
had bestowed prettiness, rather than power
for a gift.   Pink and white and flaxen
sweet-faced Claire Bailey has not a few
admirers among the male youth of the
county; yet she is very retiring and
modest, scarcely seems to recognise the
fact that she is thought pretty, and never
gives pert answers as do some of her
intimate friends and playmates.

It is evident that Claire is returning
from some errand of mercy, for she is
carrying a tin can and a basket, both of
which have once been filled with this world's
good things.   But it is scarcely probable
that Claire's poor neighbours have provided
the thoughts on which she is dwelling so

profoundly, that she does not heed the rain clouds threatening overhead, nor the electric fluid charging, almost to suffocation, the autumnal breeze. All living beings, however, are not so inactive as Claire and the insects and the birds, for a horse and rider come clattering along the road as though determined, by their example, to wake all nature into life. To a degree they succeed, for Claire returns suddenly from dreamland, and looks across the underwood dividing the path along which she is idling from the high road.

The rider stops so unexpectedly as to bring his horse almost down on his haunches. A deep blush suffuses the young girl's white brow, a blush which has not even cleared off when the man leaps off his horse, quiets the half-frightened animal, and scrambles with the bridle on his arm across the bushes to her side.

'Why, Claire, what are you doing out in this weather ? It is raining hard.'

'Is it?' And either from shyness or some other cause, she seems afraid to answer him; yet he is not such a terrible individual. Most women would have thought him a handsome young fellow. He is just five-and-twenty, tall and well made, almost an athlete in proportion, with curling brown hair and large expressive eyes. The sort of man of whom boarding-school misses would say, 'Is he not sweet?' And yet Claire — poor timid little Claire — seems afraid of him. She does find just a little voice though, to whisper flusteringly,—

'If it is raining should you not go home, or come up to the house? Mamma will be glad to see you.'

'Since when have you been so careful of my health, Miss Claire?'

The colour was deeper than ever now, the voice more inaudible.

'Have you not been very ill?'

'Oh, yes; but I have been quite well for weeks. I should have been to call on you —I mean on Lady Laura—before, only—'

The girl looked a query.

'I thought I was not wanted.'

There was a short silence, for she did not contradict him, during which Matthew Desborough gazed at the young lady with his curly head just a little on one side, and wondered. They were very old friends these two, friends from early childhood, when Matthew, who was a few years Claire's senior, used to play the part of patronising elder brother.

> To her he was
> Even as a brother—but no more ; 'twas much,
> For brotherless she was, save in the name
> Her infant friendship had bestowed upon him.

While he, as years passed on, and boyhood grew to manhood, learnt his first love lesson as he one day saw Claire's dainty feet tripping from boulder to boulder

across a stream. Matthew was an impetuous youth, and like wild-fire the new feeling
increased till its demonstrative character
frightened the timid Claire, and she said
she would have no more of Matthew Desborough for a friend—still less for a lover,
for he terrified and bewildered her. Twice
had he pleaded his suit in urgent passionate words; each time she had fled from
him like a scared lapwing to the parent
nest, and he had been compelled either
'to eat his heart' in solitude, or rush incon-
sequently into other pursuits, loving more
desperately, because thwarted in his love,
vainly seeking to forget.

The rain began to pour in torrents.
What was to be done? All chance of getting to the house without being wet through
was quite hopeless. An overhanging elm
a few yards off was the only shelter the
situation afforded. The man bade his fair
acquaintance run there at once, and began

to coax his horse through the bracken, a proceeding which the animal did not regard very kindly.

At last, however, horse and man are once more standing beside Claire, who evidently dislikes the present position of affairs quite as much as does her equine companion.

'Had I not better go home? What will mamma think?' she asks nervously.

'That you are safe in Goody Morris's cottage, where, I suppose, you have been. At any rate it is quite impossible for you to walk across the open park in such a downpour as this. I shall not think of allowing it.'

She looked up at him and smiled — probably the magisterial tone of the last part of the speech amused her. The most unqueenlike, the least pretentious of women will fain assume little airs of sovereignty when she finds herself reigning with despotic sway over an adoring lord of creation; but

she caught an expression in his eye which
made her instantly look down again and
blush as she had done once before.   Matthew
Desborough, who, it was evident, had learned
to serve two masters, since he was not only
a disciple of Lently, but also a votary of
Cupid, took her hand—somewhat of a daring
measure, all circumstances being considered ;
she did not attempt to withdraw it, however,
but stood looking very frightened and flushed.

'Can it be possible, Claire, that I am so
wholly indifferent to you as you would have
me to believe ?'

'I don't know,' she said almost inaudibly.

It was a silly answer, but it served to raise
by many degrees the thermometer of Matthew
Desborough's spirits, for he looked radiant,
and the large eyes beamed with delight.
This disciple of Lently's then could think of
earthly love, or was it from the supposed
absence of human affection that he had
become a disciple of Lently?   Who shall

say? It is a question involving many subtle
workings of the mental machinery. His next
remark, at all events, was mundane enough,
for he asked, quoting Benedict, cheerily,—

'And pray, then, now tell me for which of
my bad parts didst thou first fall in love with
me?'

The lady, however, lacked Beatrice's spirit,
for she answered very simply,—

'When I heard you were ill I was so afraid
you would die.'

'Claire!' and his arm encircled her waist
before she had time to stop it, even if she
would.

'Is it true, then, you do really love me
just a little?'

Claire's timid lips refused to utter any
more words, but she hid her face on his
shoulder, and drops fell there that came not
from the clouds above, though Matthew
Desborough deemed them heaven-sent. He
had already descended many degrees from the

summit of Lently's goodness-standard. And
thus it happened that he was a truant from
the family dinner-table, for thunder showers
do not clear off quickly, and before there was
a rainbow in the sky and a bright gleam of
happy sunshine in Claire's face, the dinner-
bell must have long since rung at Vantage
Park.

The inmates of Swanover Cottage, where
Claire and her mother, Lady Laura Bailey,
lived, were not so ambitious in their habits;
they dined at two o'clock, contenting themselves in the evening, when alone, with that
highly indigestible and especially feminine
meal—a meat tea.

About seven o'clock, when it was already
beginning to grow dusk, Matthew was carrying the can and basket, with the bridle on
his arm, giving Prig occasionally an encouraging word—though naturally the chief of his
attention was bestowed on Claire—astonish-
ing the horse, who was unaccustomed to such

vagaries on the part of his master, not a little. He was however at last in the open, when a fresh eccentricity was in store for Prig. Matthew insisted that Claire should mount him, while he led him carefully at walking pace ; the long rain-charged grass would wet her frivolous boots through in no time, he declared. Vainly she assured him they were very thick—even clumped. It was useless. Matthew, in his new position of accepted lover, would have his own way.

Lady Laura was at the drawing-room window when they arrived. She opened it, and looked at them with a half-comical, half-surprised expression on her comely face. Left a widow when she was very young, she had by no means passed the attractive age ; but she was old fashioned enough, she explained, to grow prematurely old when her husband died, and she had since then devoted herself solely to Claire, who was her idol. Perhaps there was no dearer wish in Lady Laura's heart than that her child should become Matthew Desborough's wife. She held his character in high esteem, and did not perceive the priggishness which George contemned, or the volatility of disposition of which Mr Sivewright was fully conscious. So she received them graciously, but with much tact, making no allusion to the change she instinctively felt had taken place in their mutual relations.

'Come in both of you, at once. Are you very wet?' she asked eagerly. 'I have had some fire lighted, as I thought my Claire would be cold. So good of you to put her on your horse, Matthew. Ben will take him round to the stables. Come in and tell me all your adventures.

And thus, without more words, they both went together into Lady Laura's pretty drawing-room, where Claire was petted with a mother's tenderest care, and Matthew

was not reminded that it was six months
since he had crossed the threshold of Swanover Cottage. They gave an account of
how they had accidentally met as the rain
was beginning, though it was but a bald
and halting tale at which the mother smiled.
Perhaps her imagination filled with bright
colouring the seeming weak places.

'Run away and take your hat off, Claire,
love, and then we will go into the dining-
room and see if we can't refresh this hungry
man.'

Claire wanted no second bidding. How
glad she was of five minutes' solitude, during
which she vainly strove to arrange into
some order the tumultuous feelings circling
round her heart. She had scarcely closed
the door when Matthew rushed up to Lady
Laura, and taking both her hands said
excitedly,—

'You will give me Claire, dear Lady
Laura—say you will. She has consented to

love me, and I shall take such care of her.
I shall have some money eventually, my
mother's fortune, you know; but, of course,
we sha'n't be married till I have taken
orders and—'

'Stop, my dear Matthew, not so fast—
you take my breath away. She has consented to love you, you say? That is an
odd phrase. What does it mean? I must
cross-question my little Claire. I thought
it was arranged she did not care for
you.'

'Oh, that was long ago, before she understood her own feelings.'

'And you have been trying to instruct
her in them. So, so, I must go farther
into this matter and have a talk with
Claire.'

'But if Claire wishes it you will consent,
will you not, dear Lady Laura?'

'Well, between you, I suppose I shall be
compelled. We poor chicken - pecked

mammas have no alternative but to obey. But I don't feel so sure about Claire.'

'Oh, that is all right. I am not afraid of her now if you don't object.'

'A thunder-shower seems indeed to have cleared the air,' said Lady Laura laughing, as at this moment Claire, looking very bright and happy, popped her head in at the door.

'Tea is quite ready, mamma,' but she was gone again before either her mother or Matthew had time to stop her.

The presence of the servant in the dining-room was the safeguard she sought to shelter her from the otherwise inevitable explanation. Before the homely repast was over it had proved itself unnecessary to the mother's heart.

Claire's eyes had told their own tale.

Some half-hour later Matthew was suddenly overcome by the recollection that his family would be anxious at his unusual absence. Prig was brought round from the stables, and both the ladies went out to see him mount.

'I think you may reckon on me for a coadjutrix,' said Lady Laura in a low voice, as she shook hands with him, while Claire fondled the horse, kissing his brown velvet nose with a sort of approximate affection, 'for once in your life I do believe you have read the signs aright.'

When George learns what eventful episode made his brother late for dinner, it will probably afford him even more merriment than the account of Mr Sivewright's passage-at-arms with the duke.

CHAPTER IV.

MONTARLIS CASTLE.

'HE is a duke; but he might be a cobbler,' is a stricture not infrequently passed on William, seventh Duke of Montarlis, Marquis of Suthorne, Earl of Brently, and Baron Goldford as says Burke. Sitting at the bottom of his own table, he certainly presents no very imposing appearance.

'Cunning and common,' were well chosen epithets were he an ordinary man; but he is a duke, so they are magnified into 'distinguished and discerning.'

The duke was not a young man; he was considerably over sixty before he inherited the family title, having been up to that time plain Mr Scivener, the offshoot of a very remote branch of the ducal house of Montarlis.

To a degree he was sensible of his own shortcomings, both in appearance and in the capability, for all at once assuming the position of one of England's greatest nobles. He had therefore judged it expedient to bestow his hand and dukedom on a lady who, herself but the daughter of a rich commoner, yet was well qualified in every respect to fill a duchess's place, wearing his honours with little sovereign airs, and dispensing her hospitalities with a knowledge of amalgamation and combination of which the duke was totally ignorant.

She was a white-skinned, fleshy woman, about thirty. She had been married a little over three years, and fashionable gossips said she had decidedly been fast herself before her marriage, though no one could exactly attribute any particular scandal to her name, probably from the fact that she had very quiet manners, and a 'don't understand' look in her large eyes. Be it as it might, since she had become Duchess of Montarlis, she had followed a discreet path. Perhaps she was just a little afraid of stumbling back into old habits, and had therefore selected the Rev. Lawrence Sivewright as confidant and counsellor—a strong rock on which to lean without the fear of brittle pieces breaking off at those inconvenient moments when she most wanted support. Especially since she had returned from Italy, now more than a year ago, had the duchess clung to Mr Sivewright, much to the secret dissatisfaction of Mrs Desborough, who could have forgiven everything in the 'dear duchess,' save this attempt to monopolise the vicar.

While the duchess had been abroad she had made or rather renewed acquaintance with a Mrs Tremayne, who had since then been a tolerably constant visitor at Mont-

arlis Castle. She was a widow, a year or
two younger than the duchess, in the full
zenith of attractiveness and intrigue.   A
brunette, with laughing eyes and bright
warm colouring—this fashionable, dashing
siren kept the house-party alive with her
laughter and her jokes, while the neighbours
muttered little 'Ohs!' and 'Ahs!' in sup-
pressed tones—'she was scarcely the woman
they would have imagined the duchess would
have selected for her familiar friend.' It had
been explained by the word 'playmate,' still
an uncomfortable feeling hung about the
intimacy, as though the duchess were not
altogether a free agent in the matter.

Mr Sivewright and the lady in question
constantly had little spars, owing possibly to
some degree of jealousy with which each
one regarded the other's influence in high
quarters. To Mrs Desborough, who by
some fortuitous circumstances had not yet
met Mrs Tremayne, the occasional accounts

she received of these battles were indeed treats, and she was fully prepared to worship at the Tremayne shrine when they should be introduced at the ducal dinner party.

Scarcely, however, did she expect such a bewildering little woman as the gay young widow proved, with her dazzling complexion, her brilliant eyes, her pearly teeth, and her toilette. The Maison Roger might well be proud of such a master-work of diaphanous pink—yet she sued in *formâ pauperis*, asking always for indulgence in her vain efforts to vie with ducal riches.

'It is so dreadful to have rich friends. I am at my wits' end ; and quite at my purses' end too for the matter of that,' she had confided to Mrs Desborough when, the long dinner being over, they were sitting having a little woman's talk before the advent of the gentlemen.

'I am always telling dear Julia she should let me go back to my doll's house, for I have a doll's house of my own. Oh! it *is* tiny. However, if Julia wants me, of course I must remain for the sake of auld lang syne. Heigho!'

And fringed lashes veiled her dazzling eyes, but for all that she failed to look subdued or sentimental. For a second or two Mrs Desborough had time to wonder what it all meant. Then Mrs Tremayne looked up once more, and the flush came back.

'Isn't Julia handsome? And doesn't she look every inch a duchess. I always said she was born for an exalted position instead of—'

Mrs Desborough looked a query.

'A miserable, petty lot like mine,' went on the chatterbox, whose first idea had obviously been a different one.

'I admire the duchess immensely,' Mrs Desborough began. 'There is something so very distinguished in her bearing, and she is so very—'

'Chic, cachet, and all that sort of thing—yes,' and Mrs Tremayne laughed rippingly; 'particularly when you compare her with her surroundings. This room is a perfect museum of oddities. Do tell me who some of them are.'

'The lady in black with the dried-up face is Mrs Lancelot Cairns; the girl in brown is her daughter. They are very worthy people—do an immense amount of good.'

'Do they? What a pity they ever leave off. I am sure they are doing no good here. And the bright green woman by the piano? I hope she is not going to sing.'

'She is a Miss Chiffonal. Her father sat by you at dinner.'

'Just so. He drew me; was it not bad luck? Do you like the practice here of drawing lots for your dinner partner? It is rather fun standing at the door with the hat. I feel as if I was making a *quête* in

a church—in fact, it is the only time that
I ever feel really good.'

'I think I like the old plan of precedence
best,' observed Mrs Desborough. 'This
one must inevitably lead to a good deal of
ill-feeling.'

'Squabbles without end. I'll tell you
such an amusing one. Mr Sivewright was
the hero. You know Mr Sivewright, of
course ?'

Mrs Desborough's soft laces fluttered.

'Our very dear vicar. Certainly I know
Mr Sivewright.'

'Ah! Naturally you and he would sym-
pathise; but he does not approve of me.
I shock him. I have had an odd education,
Mrs Desborough, or rather none at all. I
was dragged up in a sort of fashion.'

'Were you brought up in France ?'

'Well, yes, partly,' and Mrs Tremayne
laughed. 'But never mind that. A few
nights ago when your vicar was dining

here he drew me. I saw it as plainly as if Violet Tremayne had been written on his brow. Of course, he thought that luck would be sure to favour a parson in the game of speculation, and that he would draw the duchess.'

This time Mrs Desborough's lace grew ruffled, and little points seemed to show themselves.

'Well, our mutual friend walked away without uttering a word, and left me to finish my partner-lottery. The last straggler, a man they call Adonis Valmont, came in just before the dinner was announced. I presented him with the last ticket and put down the hat. Too much engaged in twisting his moustache to look at his paper, he sauntered on to the hearthrug when I saw—actually saw—him change it with Mr Sivewright for coin—half-a-crown, I believe. It was the duchess—that I also saw on Mr Sivewright's face.'

' " Bribery and corruption," I said, walking up to him, " are not permitted. I am the genius of the hat." '

' " And I have the honour of taking you into dinner," said Adonis Valmont.'

' " No, Mr Valmont, I decline ; you are to take the duchess. Give back that half-crown ; we are not going to be bought and sold like merchandise. Come, Mr Sivewright, I'll answer for it—you shall be punished here if you think you won't be there," pointing downwards of course.'

Mrs Desborough laughed and looked very beaming, though of course she protested.

' Mr Sivewright could not do such a thing,' she said.

' He'll do anything not to be bored,' answered the other ; ' and there is no mistake about the fact he was bored that night. I would not even argue with him ; I never spoke, and he had got a deaf mummy on the other side. I hope he liked it, anyhow he will not throw me over again, and the next time he draws me I shall decline to go with him, if I go to bed without my dinner.'

'So it is war to the knife between you and the vicar. I did not know he was of so belligerent a turn. Do you really dislike him?'

'I? No. He is a sort of clerical anomaly that amuses me; but I never put up with slights from men—but here come the gentlemen. I'll go and sing them in before Miss Chiffonal gets possession of the instrument.'

And in a second or two the atmosphere of the room seemed filled with ripples from Violet Tremayne's liquid voice.

Mr Sivewright dropped into the vacant place by Mrs Desborough.

'How beautifully she sings; how charming she is,' said the lady. She felt she could afford to praise.

'Yes, but she is too overpowering—a restless, excitable woman. She has no repose. She does not understand the present moment; enjoyment with her consists in anticipating what is going to happen in an hour. I don't think I ever met any one who tried all my senses like Mrs Tremayne.'

'Who was she?'

Mr Sivewright shrugged his shoulders. 'She is not in Burke, I fancy. She and the duchess knew each other as girls; it is almost a pity they met again.'

'They are of very different natures, hence the sympathy, I presume,' said Mrs Desborough in a little prim way she had at times.

'Perhaps; the duchess decidedly gains by the contrast. Oh! how infinitely I prefer quiet reposeful women. There is something so much more sympathetic about them. Look at the duchess as she moves now from one to another of her guests. Queen-like, swan-

like, undulating—that is the perfection of
feminine grace ; and that clinging white
satin—see how it sets off the contour of
her figure.'

'Are you joking, Mr Sivewright ?' asked
Mrs Desborough, to whom these rhapsodies
on another woman's charms were most unpleasing. It was the first time too, the
vicar had ever talked to her in this strain ;
but on this occasion he had sat very near
the duchess at dinner, and the duke's cham-
pagne was of the best. Nor did Mrs Desborough's frowns deter him from persisting
in the assertion that 'her grace of Montarlis was a magnificent woman—a mon-
strous fine woman.'

Yes, she had chosen wisely when she had
selected the Rev. Lawrence Sivewright for
an ally, and Mrs Desborough was beginning to fear that her longer friendship with
the vicar was crumbling away from its very
antiquity — for that probably her twenty

years of priority in age were beginning to
tell.   Mrs Desborough had, however, learned
the discretion of silence ; only by the sharp
quick movement of her face were her feelings visible.   After a second she recovered
herself completely, and smiled benignly
on the vicar.   During that second she had
resolved to hold her ground, and perhaps
she thought a tilt with a duchess were no
mean warfare.

' In matters of taste you are infallible,' she
said blandly.   ' No one can gainsay that
the duchess is beautiful—to-night looking
more than usually so—and that she has
wonderfully good style ; but still, for all that,
I am vastly taken with Mrs Tremayne's
laughing face and laughing manners.   She
is like a beam of sunshine on a winter's
day.'

Thus it was clearly manifest that Mrs
Desborough had the intention to cultivate
the acquaintance of Violet Tremayne, and

through her means to strengthen the intimacy between Montarlis Castle and Vantage Park.

Always be on the most sociable and loving terms with people of whom you have sufficient fear to be jealous.

Mrs Desborough had lived long enough in the world, and studied its ways sufficiently close, to be thoroughly cognisant of this fact. Her patience with Mr Sivewright in his present mood, however, was nearly exhausted—though she did not wish to show it—so she got up and walked towards the piano, meeting her hostess half way across the room.

'Dear duchess, that charming friend of yours is too delightful ; and how she sings !'

'Yes. Violet is a good little thing, and is always ready to please and be useful.'

But the duchess's brow clouded as though praise bestowed, even by a woman, on Violet Tremayne were scarcely pleasing to her.

'Will you drive over to luncheon, and

bring her with you some day soon?' went
on Mrs Desborough. 'You have not been
to see me for so long.'

'Yes, with pleasure, it will be something
new for Violet; she is always craving for
new excitements.'

'George has come home,' said Mrs Desborough.   'And the dear boy has no end
of funny stories—some of them very amusing.'

'Indeed! George is a great favourite of
mine.   He is so fresh and racy.   I am sorry
I did not know.   I should have asked him
to come to-night.   Shall we say Tuesday
for luncheon?   Tell your son I shall count
on his being at home.'

Mrs Desborough was radiant.   She could
not guess the thought that lay beneath
that serene voice; it had its existence
nevertheless.

'If only George Desborough would marry
Violet Tremayne.'

CHAPTER V.

THE CHURCH OR THE HOME.

'HALTE la! impetuous youth.' And Matthew, who was walking with rapid strides down the carriage drive at Vantage Park, found himself suddenly arrested by the appearance of an umbrella in front of him.

'Ah! Mr Sivewright, I was going to call on you.'

'Indeed!' and the vicar's eyebrows arched. It was not often Matthew turned his steps towards Fernwood Vicarage.

'Yes ; I did not wish you to hear of my engagement to Miss Bailey from any one else.'

'Your engagement to Miss Bailey ? Mrs

Desborough did not tell me,' and the vicar looked as surprised as a man of his calibre could permit himself to look.

'No, no; my mother does not approve. Besides, I begged her to be silent for the present. But you do not congratulate me.'

'My dear Matthew, to see you comfortably ensconced as paterfamilias in some snug country parsonage were indeed a matter for congratulation could I believe it possible; but I thought you were vowed to celibacy and all that sort of thing.'

'Not at all—not at all. If such were my views I might as well go to Rome at once.'

'Oh! I don't pretend to have a lens sufficiently clear to detect the miscroscopic line which defines the boundaries of the two faiths. In my private opinion it is non-existent—a mere optical delusion.'

'One must be allowed to exercise a little private judgment, pleaded Matthew, 'whereas in Rome—'

' Pooh ! nonsense, my dear young friend.
There is no middle way—faith or reason.
As soon as you begin to exercise the latter
the first disappears. You are only cheating
yourself by trying to take the kernels out
of both nuts. A married father-confessor
is an anomaly, though, if you follow my
advice, you'll stick to matrimony, and give
up all this new-fangled nonsense.'

' You forget that Claire entertains the same
views.'

' Oh ! yes, silly children both of you. You'll
grow wiser as you grow older. Your mother
does not approve of the marriage, you say,
and wherefore ?'

' She thinks we are both too young, and,
moreover, upon my word I hardly like to tell
you, but, in short, she hints that it is the
result of some manœuvre on the part of Lady
Laura.'

' While it is entirely a matter of spontaneous
combustion, eh ? Well, I must have a few

words with Mrs Desborough on the subject.'

'You will—you will tell her that you think
it highly, intensely advantageous for us both ;
that it would be cruel and unkind to do anything to prevent it.'

'Stop, stop ! I am not going to pledge myself to any wild extravagancies. It is more
probable that you will have to bring a little
more common sense to bear on the acts of
your daily life. Fewer visions and more real
practical working will be expected from a
man who has saddled himself with the onus
of matrimony.'

' Not even for Claire can I deny my faith,'
said Matthew fervently.

'Your faith ! Well, well, well, we shall see
which is stronger, love or fear.'

And Mr Sivewright leant gracefully against
a rustic seat which chanced to be close by.

' Fear, Mr Sivewright, fear ! What do you
mean ? '

' It is excessive selfishness that makes all you fellows so perverse and argumentative. If you were not afraid of eternal punishment you would talk in a very different strain.'

' And are not you afraid of eternal punishment, Mr Sivewright ? ' and Matthew looked horrified and aghast.

' I ? I hope I have too unbounded a belief in the power and goodness and wonderful benevolence of Heaven.'

' Perhaps you don't think we shall be punished at all ? '

Mr Sivewright shrugged his shoulders.

' Let each follow his own conscience, and trim, to the best of his power, the lamp which illumes it, and don't let us trouble our heads about an unknown future, which is more inexplorable than even the Arctic regions to which, by the way, do you observe a new Government expedition is about to start ? '

' More energy is displayed in connection

with the things of this life than about the
great matters of eternity!' exclaimed Matthew fiercely. He was very irate at what
he considered Mr Sivewright's levity.

'And yet the great Creator gave us to
enjoy, or why this beautiful earth, these riches
of nature and art by which we are surrounded ?
Your creed seems to me so suppressive of
all natural enjoyment, that if for no other
reason I should condemn it. It is no use
to set our religious standard too high, my
young friend ; we are but human, and are
apt to get dizzy on a height. You are at this
moment in danger of toppling over ; Claire
versus Creed—something of a desperate conflict I expect. Of course you will follow Mr
Lently's advice, so I will withhold any farther
counsel for the present, and go and pay my
respects to Mrs Desborough.'

And they parted, the vicar muttering to
himself —

'Wise woman, Mrs Desborough ; but who

so wise as a woman in diplomacy? She thwarts this boy because, forsooth, she wishes him to marry. I have taken the cue, I think, and Lently will find a restive pupil when next he and Master Matthew regale themselves with a little disputation.'

The vicar was right. He had sown the seeds of discord in Matthew's mind, for he too went muttering down the avenue,—

'Why should I not marry? Who has any right to stop me? Am I not a free agent? Lently—Sivewright—what bosh! I shall do as I please. I shall see Lently at once and tell him what I think. He is married. Bother Sivewright! he is always so consumedly satirical.'

So, instead of the ceremonious visit which Matthew felt himself in duty bound to pay to the old family friend, when he got outside the park gates he vaulted a stile, crossed some fields with hasty steps, walked a good half-mile down a rutty green lane, then over

some more fields, till the spire of a pretty
village church was visible, and close to the
church a gabled parsonage-house, snugly
built among elm trees.

Ravensholme Vicarage was less pretentious than its sister of Fernwood, but it was
homely and comfortable-looking, if only its
internal arrangements had not contradicted
external signs.

As Matthew approached, screams from
young voices met his ears—not the happy
joyous yells of exulting childhood, but the
discordant, hideous outcry of spoiled, un-
manageable, discontented brats.   Matthew
was a privileged individual ; he had free
admission at all hours into Ravensholme
Vicarage, and he used it now, for he walked
straight in at the back-door, and came
abruptly on the scene of the affray.

Mrs Lently—for the Rev. Luke, notwithstanding his tendencies, was a married
man—Mrs Lently was standing slipshod, in

a state of greasy *déshabillé*, among her pro-
geny, who were all squalling round her,
while she strove vainly to raise her voice in
angry tones, so as to be heard above the
general uproar.   Neither her own un-
groomed condition nor the generally unruly
state of the establishment seemed, however,
to affect her, for she turned to Matthew
with a smile on her broad, kindly face,—

'Quiet them for me, Mr Matthew, will
you ? You are the only one who can.'

These words were conveyed more by signs
than sound, for the youngsters' clamour increased when they saw Matthew, who very
frequently indulged them in a game of romps.

At the present moment, however, his mind
was too much bent on his own affairs to be
very indulgent for the little Lentlys' shortcomings.

' I'd smack every white head of you if I
were your mother,' he said sharply. ' Cease
this din instantly, or I'll never race you round

the garden again, or take you up to the park
to climb the mulberry tree.'

Matthew looking angry was an unusual
sight, and so impressed the children that they
left off howling to stare at him.

Master Bobbie, a four-year-old, was the
first to break the silence. With his thumb
well in his mouth he heaved a deep sigh,
while two tears stopped half way down his
cheeks, as though they too wondered what
had happened, and when he had looked at
Matthew for a few seconds, he said senten-
tiously,—' Bobbie bad boy ! Bobbie must go
to black place. Bobbie be dood for sweets.'

Matthew turned from the group of children and looked out of the window.

' Bribery and fear,' he repeated to himself.

How unbidden thoughts will force themselves — how involuntary is at times the
action of the mind ; his recent conversation
with Mr Sivewright was paramount.

But the children having speedily recovered

their natural buoyancy, clamoured round him
for play, and thus disputed the possession of
him with his thoughts. For a few minutes
they were successful ; but Matthew's feelings
had been too deeply stirred for him to lay
them long on one side at infantine bidding.

Mrs Lently perhaps noticed a pre-occupied
look on his brow, for she rang the bell. A
maid, wearing earrings and dirty ribands,
answered the summons.

'Take them all away Susan, every one,'
said the mistress pettishly.

This order was the signal for another out-
break from the youngsters ; but among much
weeping and kicking and shrieking they
were at last conveyed, to Matthew's no small
satisfaction, to the nursery.

'Mr Lently is out. Do you want to see
him ?' asked the lady, as soon as the door
was closed.

Out ! of course he was. What man could
stand such a household ? So instead of his

club he took to what he called parochial
work. Stop a moment though. Reverse
the picture. May it not be because he is
always out that his home has become a
pandemonium? And when he does come in
his martyr-like appearance and general con-
demnation of everything that is pleasant or
cheery do not contribute largely to the
gaiety of the establishment. He married
when he was very young a woman some
years older than himself. They were ill-
assorted in every way. He was unpractical,
visionary, and theoretical; while she was a
pretty doll, plastic in mind as the wax from
which her body seemed to have been moulded.
Mrs Lently would have followed any path that
had been shown her clearly and practically;
but she was totally incapable of selecting one
for herself, and failed utterly in reaching her
husband's high flights. In the early part of
their married life he had spread his pinions
and soared above the earth in a good many

different directions, till he had at last flapped his wings into the Ritualistic course. His wife tried to accompany him, but after several futile attempts she floundered hopelessly.

There were the children, the dreadful servants, the house-bills, the mendings, the cleanings, and, worse than all, there was an incompetent head that never could arrange the simplest plan or carry out unassisted the merest trifle. So Mrs Lently never found time to go to her husband's week-day services, but led an untidy tangled life, in which nothing was begun at the beginning or finished up to the end; and while the Rev. Luke Lently's church decorations and services were remarked on as more ambitious and advanced than those of any other divine in those parts ; while his teaching, in spite of his belief in purgatory, left no middle way for imperfection, his home afforded a theme for speculation, and made people remark how fre-

quently experiment fails to prove theory. All
his neighbours admitted readily that Mrs
Lently was a well-intentioned, simple-minded
woman, and it was weakness of purpose, not
vicious inclination, that made her a slattern
and a peevish whining grumbler.

For natures such as hers, the Rev. Luke
Lently's religious code had not provided.
She never even succeeded in understanding
the dogmas he was perpetually enumerating ;
so she contented herself with setting him
down in her own private calendar as a
saint, and following the cursory unmethodi-
cal way of her own very earthly life, nag-
ging off the roughest bits by means of her
tongue, as though the sound of her own
voice were a consolation to her.

Matthew Desborough and Mrs Lently
were on very friendly terms. He himself
was somewhat halting in determination, and
he had consequently a certain amount of
fellow-feeling for her shortcomings, not unfre-

quently doing her a good turn in the way of helping her out of some difficulty, about which the great Lently would not have allowed himself to be troubled. He had not, however, sufficient respect for her sagacity to make her his confidante on this occasion, scorching though the words were which burnt his tongue impatient to be uttered.

He walked up and down the room excitedly, every now and then fidgeting with the things on the mantel-shelf or table in a way that would have made most women chide him ; but Mrs Lently was accustomed to Matthew's vagaries. She took no notice, only chatted on in a maudlin sort of way about the petty worries of her every-day existence, and gave the usual *catalogue raisonée* of children, servants, breakages, butcher's bills, etcetera. She was interrupted at last by a sudden question from Matthew.

' Does Lently ever go to Lady Laura
Bailey's ? '

' Yes, sometimes, I think ; and Miss
Bailey comes here pretty often, and is so
nice with the children. She used to come
here every day when you were ill. It is
a pity you have quarrelled with the Baileys,
Mr Matthew.'

He coloured up, and answered rapidly,—

' Who said I had quarrelled with them ?
Why did you not tell me Claire had been
here ? '

' Oh ! because she told me not. I can't
think how it slipped out now, but I am a
poor thing at keeping a secret. She is so
good. Do you remember when the children
had measles, and then Jane took them too,
and cook had a bad leg. There was I left
as usual without a living being to do the
work, and Luke saying I ought to go to
church at eight, and again in the afternoon.
Of course I know I ought, but how could

I? It's only idle people that will get to Heaven if church is to take them there— that is what I tell Luke; but of course he is a saint; he can't understand my difficulties.'

'Well, and Claire Bailey?' interrupted Matthew.

'Oh! she came and helped me—actually made puddings and gruel for the babies with her own hands. Ah! I wish I was like Miss Bailey. The place used to look quite different after she had been here an hour or so. But I never could be tidy. My poor mother used to say—'

'And Claire came every day and did these things? Where was I?'

'Oh! you were ill, and then you went abroad. I don't suppose you ever even heard of the trouble we were in here. I don't know what I should have done without that angel, for Luke is nothing at—'

'And Claire was not afraid of catching

the measles?' asked Matthew, anxious to keep Mrs Lently from wandering.

'Not she. When is she ever afraid for herself when there is good to be done? I had hoped, Mr Matthew, that you and she—'

'Is not that Lently coming along the road?'

And Matthew was suddenly desirous to change the subject, for he perceived that it was growing personal.

'Yes, that it is; and, good gracious! he had no breakfast before he went out. He said he would have it at twelve. It is now half-past, and I've forgotten to tell the cook.'

And away went Mrs Lently to see what sort of an uncomfortable repast could be concocted at a minute's notice for her hungry husband.

CHAPTER VI.

MR LENTLY'S CROSS.

MR LENTLY'S private study is small, paper strewn and unorderly, the latter being the characteristic disposition of everything at Ravensholme Vicarage, both mentally and materially. His sanctum has, however, the merit of being a quiet nook, as far removed as possible from nursery clamour; while a side door opening on to a little path which leads directly from the garden to the church renders the Rev. Luke an independent agent in his exits and entrances.

Matthew is sitting there now, his legs stretched out, his hands clasped together, his brows flushed, his eyes flashing ; in fact there are decidedly feverish tendencies exhibiting themselves, and considering how ill he had been a few months back, his mother, and probably Claire, would have thought his present state a highly dangerous one ; but the Rev. Luke Lently has no such scruples, as with a stern look on his ascetic brow he is, to all appearance, holding the knife firmly which is to eradicate what he calls the hankering after worldliness in his young friend and disciple. He is, however, but one of those bungling operators who slash without science. Mr Lently is inflicting a desperate wound which fails nevertheless to touch the supposed disease ; he has reckoned too much on his patient's belief in his advice, without which belief it is said that no real cure is ever effected. Weak natures are not necessarily the most plastic by reason of the very obstinacy that is in them, and for this strongly-developed feature in the neophyte

he thought all his own he had not calculated. Ah ! the Rev. Lawrence Sivewright,
whatever his shortcomings in matters of
faith, possessed undoubtedly the larger share
of acumen ; there were few dispositions,
whatever their peculiar proclivities, that he
was incapable of bending if it pleased him
to make the attempt. A pity the gift were
not bestowed on a holier man, it had been
observed, but the laws of compensation are
very evenly balanced, and the gift was in
itself a trial—a burden on that conscience
Mr Sivewright was always striving so manfully to follow—for was there not hidden
away somewhere in his heart a whispering
fear lest, in influencing people to his views, he
was corrupting them to evil ? for that which
seemed truth to him might scarcely fill the
void in another soul. But to waive digression.

Matthew's last remark, whatever it was,
had roused the usually dormant irascibility
which was latent in Mr Lently's nature. He

had been writing for some time with his back turned to his pupil, occasionally writing and occasionally enunciating his dogmas in a phlegmatic sort of way, which, to say the least, was irritating. At this juncture he turned suddenly round and faced the younger man.

'Marry, marry if you will, but renounce at once all claim to ever becoming a true priest. We want no more married clergy to choke up the ranks of the Anglican Church.'

Matthew rose, and stood looking doggedly at his opponent.

'I shall marry, of that I am resolved, and I shall take orders too, if it so pleases me when the time comes. I was wrong perhaps to have consulted you, since your own married life seems to have been a mistake.'

'Every married life is a mistake, when a man's first mistress is the Church,' answered Mr Lently.

'I cannot see any difficulty in the combination of Church and marriage,' pursued Matthew; 'it works very well in many instances.'

'Claire Bailey, forsooth! Claire Bailey to be set up against our holy mother Church! Give her up Matthew, give her up as you value your immortal soul.'

'Pooh, nonsense, Mr Lently, you are mad. You of all men to talk like this.'

'It is because I am what I am that I do talk thus. Do you think my life is not one endless penance for past foolishness. You know better than any man that my home is anything but a happy one, that wife and children rise in continual rebellion against my views and feelings. It is my cross, Matthew, the cross I have had to bear—shall bear to the end—avoid it, my young friend, avoid it. If you have the strength of Samson, it will crush you with its weight.'

Matthew thought of the two pilgrims who started on their pilgrimage with peas in their shoes, and how the one who took the precaution to boil his peas arrived with speedy steps and fresh mien at the goal, while the other lagged behind footsore and weary ; but he had too much respect for his pastor to point the allegory, he merely observed quietly, his impatience abating as that of Mr Lently increased.

'There are various ways of governing a household. Because you and Mrs Lently do not understand each other, it does not follow that every couple should be equally mis-mated.'

'It is not the case in point, not the case in point,' thundered the Rev. Luke ; 'it is marriage that is a mistake, not the fact of being linked to any particular woman. A married priest brings a curse down on his house which no prayers nor penances can remove.'

'Yet St Paul writing to Timothy, says that "a bishop should be the husband

of one wife—having his children in sub-
jection with all gravity. For if a man
know not how to rule his own house,
how shall he take care of the church of
God ?"'

Mr Lently turned once more to his writing,
and then after a second or two, as though he
thought a pause would make his words more
effective, he said slowly,—

' For they are virgins. These follow the
Lamb whithersoever He goeth.'—Rev. xiv. 4.

Matthew bit his nails. He had joined the
Ritualistic phalanx in order, as he had hinted
to Mr Sivewright, to combine ultra faith with
its equivalent in self-will, and this determined
opposition to his wishes he felt by no means
inclined to tolerate. Yet what was to be
done ? It was unreasonable and preposterous
to expect him to give up Claire, while to turn
renegade was equally impossible. No, he
must bring all the obstinacy which contradiction had awakened within him to bear on the

matter, and follow the promptings of his own inclination.

'You then really consider that marriage, under the circumstances in which I am placed, would be sin?' he asked more for the sake of receiving a definite answer from Mr Lently, than from any intention of being biassed by the same.

'Unquestionably, and one which you will have to expiate by severe penance.'

'I accept the penance,' said Matthew very quietly; 'it were worth countless penances to win Claire.'

Boanerges could be restrained no longer, he rose and began to pace the tiny room excitedly, waving his hands and arms at times in violent gesticulation, while he declaimed at his disciple as though he were practising for platform oratory.

'Is this the result of all my teaching—one more cross that I am called on to bear—to see the strong firm earth on which I had hoped your feet rested crumbling away beneath the weight of worldliness? You who I had hoped were called to be a saint, if not a martyr, for the good cause, succumbing so soon to the lust of the flesh. Oh, Matthew, return while there is yet time to your first love. "*Behold, thou art fair, my love; behold, thou art fair; thou hast doves' eyes. Behold, thou art fair, my beloved, and comely; our bed is flourishing. The beams of our house are of cedar, our rafters of cypress trees.*" Ah, is she not fair, fairer than the love of woman, our dear and holy mother Church, to whom you gave your first affections, the virgin aspirations of a young and guileless heart? And now, before the bride you had selected has even received your vows and granted you all the blessings she alone can grant, you have fallen from your first determination to love her alone in all her purity, her beauty, and her grace, and you would already share the adoration you had once re-

solved to bestow individually on her with a
frail, sinning daughter of Eve. Ah! if you
only know how I have regretted—regretted
with shudderings and tears, the web I have
woven round my own life, although I am fully
aware that I had not seen the truth in all
its fulness when I took this step. This, this is
my only chance of atonement ; but to plunge
wilfully, knowingly, into the flagrant sin of
disobedience, were an act from which he
who would lead a holy life must turn with
horror, and from which I would pray—pray
fervently, my dear Matthew, that you may
be spared. Remember, too, every one who
sins extends the image of his sin far beyond
the sphere of his personal presence. An
example of this nature would not fail to pro-
duce such a generation of increasing sin
that he who sets it becomes the ancestor, so
to speak, of a vast multitude of disobedient
and erring souls. Believe me, the truest
way to aid the faith which you profess is

to suffer for that faith : resist then, I conjure
you, without farther hesitation, this temptation to backsliding—hold firm to your earlier
determination, become, God willing, a faithful
striving priest, and never let the reproach,
hurled at the Church of Ephesus, be hurled
against you, " *Behold, I have somewhat against
thee, because thou hast left thy first love.*" '

While this avalanche of words was falling
on him with such swiftness that they were
as one crushing blow, Matthew stood passively wondering. He was used to Mr
Lently's high flights and somewhat theatrical tirades ; but he could not bring his mind
to think that the present occasion warranted
the amount of fervour displayed by the over-
zealous pastor. When so many clergy were
married, why should he be selected as the
victim to be offered on the shrine of celibacy ; but to ask Mr Lently such a question in his present mood would, he felt, be
worse than useless, so he contented himself

with saying very quietly for him—Matthew being, as we know, a youth of a hasty, passionate temperament,—

'Your words have scarcely convinced me, but I will take counsel of my own mind, and let you know the result.'

It was evident the Rev. Luke had lost ground—not gained it. A week ago Matthew would not have presumed to dispute his opinion, but would have accepted with blind obedience any dogma, however authoritative, he had sought to impose.

Mr Lently was about to commence a second portion of his wordy discourse, but Matthew took up his hat.

'Please, Mr Lently, no more to-day. I have received as much as I can digest, and having been, moreover, wounded to the quick, I must beg for breathing space to recover my mental equilibrium.'

This was scarcely a flattering response to the Rev. Luke's earnest appeal, but he bore it unflinchingly — perhaps he had enough good sense left to recognise that sufficient difficulties had been thrown in Matthew's path—for he only said very unctuously,—

'God be with you, my dear young brother, and give you light by prayer and fasting to discover the truth, and, having done all, to stand.'

And so they parted, Matthew, his soft felt hat well pulled over his brows, rolled rather than walked with unsteady gait along the homeward path, for the interview through which he had just passed had fevered his brain and convulsed his reason as though it had possessed the qualities of a potent and exciting draught. Suddenly, he stopped and considered. To go back to Vantage and be cross-questioned was, he felt, quite impossible at this moment. Claire's sweet eyes reading into his soul were equally difficult to answer. No, solitude was his only chance of regaining the composure he so

much required, and he turned into a side
walk through a wood, and let his feelings
rage at will, while he

> ' Listened to the wind that now did stir
> About the crisped oaks full drearily ;
> Yet with as sweet a softness as might be
> Remembered for its velvet summer song.'

And while Matthew dreamt, time passed
on, till growing weary perhaps of his own
unsettled train of thought, he roused himself with an effort and tried to force himself back into actual and active life.   He
had been stumbling backwards and forwards,
striving to define right and wrong to the
satisfaction of his own conscience, till he
had become as illogical as a woman.   It was
useless to pursue the subject farther for the
nonce.   He would go home and restore his
jaded frame with food.   What an unpoetical
ending to the contemplation of a difficult
love problem ! Nature, however, was stronger
in Matthew Desborough than romance, and
nature demanded alimentary sustenance.

He arrived at home about four o'clock by a little gate which opened on to the flower garden from a copse; perhaps he hoped in this way to reach the house without meeting any of his family, if so, he was destined to be disappointed, for George's cheery voice called out,—

' Hullo, Mat, playing truant again; we were thinking of having you *tambouriné*, as they do in France,' and before he could avoid a meeting Matthew found himself in the midst of a gay party, consisting of the Duchess of Montarlis, Mrs Tremayne, Mr Sivewright, his mother and brother.

Escape was impossible, so there was no alternative but to conceal as well as he could his mental agitation, and join in the conversation which was going on. ' From possessing usually an excitable manner, he succeeded in hiding from every one, excepting Mr Sivewright, the fact of the general mental overthrow under which he was labouring ; but the Rev.

Lawrence was far too acute a physiognomist not to read as in an open book the thoughts as they passed flightily through Matthew's brain, and he had no difficulty in supplying all the harassing conflicts through which his mind had passed since their interview in the morning. Mr Sivewright was sorry for Matthew,—he regretted that so much mistaken zeal should be thrown away on bubbles —and, both for his own and his mother's sake, he would have taken an unusual amount of trouble to save the young man the painful ordeal through which he saw his mind was passing. He must go home, think the matter carefully out, and then have an interview with Mrs Desborough,—and for this reason he declined to remain for dinner, warmly though he was pressed both by the lady of the house and her son George; 'he had important business,' he said, 'which would employ his entire evening.'

And so a few minutes after the duchess and Violet Tremayne had been packed into the pony carriage and had started for Montarlis, Mr Sivewright took his leave, giving Matthew so friendly a handshake as to bring the warm colour into his cheeks, though little perhaps recked he how much more the issues of his future life lay in the hands of Mr Sivewright than in those of the Rev. Luke Lently, his chosen director.

Mr Sivewright's power lay in the immense capability he had for weighing the equivalents of life, an art in which Mr Lently and Matthew both utterly failed.

'Est modus in rebus ; sunt certi denique fines
Quos ultra citraque requit consistere rectum,'

he murmured to himself, quoting his beloved Horace as he walked towards the vicarage.

This probably was the text of a sermon he was preparing for Matthew.

To men of Mr Sivewright's school, a text is not necessarily biblical.

CHAPTER VII.

ADVICE.

IT is quite true — Matthew has engaged himself to Claire Bailey. I had hoped he would listen to reason and have told no one, not even you,' and Mrs Desborough's laces were very much agitated as she fidgeted from side to side, vainly struggling into a comfortable corner for a talk with the vicar.

'Engaged—but not married,' said the vicar smiling—'there seem to be difficulties.'

'Indeed there are—my husband can't allow him enough to provide for a wife and family—and though, I am sorry to say, he must inherit my fortune, still I am not dead yet Mr Sivewright,' and the lady looked sufficiently instinct with life to be accepted as only forty by any life insurance company in the kingdom.

Mr Sivewright bowed and smiled again—the mother was in a spiteful mood, and Mrs Desborough's spiteful moods invariably made the Rev. Lawrence more unctuous —besides, he had thought the matter out since yesterday, and knew exactly the view he meant to take of the case—than which there is no stronger weapon for argument.

'You object to Claire for a daughter-in-law; but not to Matthew marrying any-one else, I presume?' he asked, but more as though he was stating a fact than asking a question.

'To Claire—yes, of course I object to Claire. I suppose you know why?'

'Matthew tells me you think them both too young.'

' Pooh, nonsense—that is mere fiction. I object to Claire, because she is Lady Laura's daughter, and it has been *guerre à outrance* between Lady Laura and me ever since we were girls. She always put herself in some objectionable form between me and the thing I most wanted—even did her utmost with her usual sly deceit to lure from me Mr Desborough's affection.'

The vicar's head turned just a little on one side bent into the least perceptible of nods : he was not quite prepared to give full credence to this statement—having always understood that Mrs Desborough had cleverly manœuvred for the squire, who had been, in the first place, more inclined to admire Lady Laura. It was not that Mrs Desborough was purposely prevaricating to the vicar. She had asserted this fact so frequently both to herself and to other people that she had ended by sincerely and firmly believing it. For years, by a consistent series of snubs and petty rudenesses conferred on the inhabitants of Swanover Cottage, she had acted up to her belief, for the circumstance that Mr Desborough was always very polite, as she observed 'quite affectionate to those Bailey's'—had the effect of some irritant poison on his wife's nature. More particularly was she annoyed at this juncture, for though he did not approve of the fact of Matthew marrying at all, he could not be coerced into giving it as his opinion that a marriage with Claire was especially objectionable.

Thus it may be inferred that for the last ten days, in fact ever since Matthew and Claire had walked together in the wood, with no other chaperone than Prig, the general tone at Vantage Park had been inharmonious and full of jars; now, however, that the vicar had undertaken to accord the various tuneless instruments, perhaps the home-concert would show a little symphony.

'The sins of the mother being visited on the daughter, eh?' he said with a half jocular expression; but if he meant to joke Mrs Desborough into a good humour, he was quite unsuccessful, for the latent venom of her nature exhibited itself virulently.

'Claire is a half-educated doll!' she said, 'with no cleverness about her, except a talent for manœuvring, which she has inherited from her mother.'

'Humph! I have not altogether understood the situation, it seems. I always fancied you wished Matthew to marry, and were therefore simply raising objections in order to make him more anxious to do so. You are aware that I consider marriage to be the only thing that will sever him from the fanatical set with whom he has lately become involved.'

'Marriage, yes—with anyone but Claire Bailey. I would rather see him an Anglican Monk, much as I despise the body, than married to her.'

'Just so; then Mr Lently had better take the case in hand. Poor Matthew—if I am not mistaken Lently has already been sowing the seeds of much tribulation in his mind.'

'And you, Mr Sivewright, one of my greatest friends, you actually mean that you are inclined to promote this marriage of Matthew into the family of my bitterest—' she broke off with a little gulp, and catching up her words, went on in a higher key, 'Oh, it is too unkind, too dispiriting, to find that everybody is against me.'

'My dear Mrs Desborough, what can it matter to me whom Matthew marries, except as far as my personal interest in you is concerned; all I say is, marriage is the only chance of his ever seeing life from a realistic

point of view, and giving up all the ideal
nonsense with which his head has of late
been crammed. However, as you seem
so strongly to object to this alliance, there
is only one alternative—send him away.
Matthew is impressionable, and by this
means you may—I don't say you will—succeed in forcing his ideas into another channel,
and making him break fresh ground, over
which neither Lently's teaching nor Claire
Bailey's dainty feet have ever passed.'

' You were born a diplomat !' exclaimed
Mrs Desborough, from whose face all the
malice had suddenly cleared. ' Unfold your
plan—I am all attention,' and she smoothed
the laces, and turned down any points which
seemed to bristle.

' The whole thing will require very judi-
cious management, my dear friend,' and the
Rev. Lawrencel ooked important and grand.
' Matthew's is no ordinary character. I
have studied it in every detail since he was

quite a lad. He must be induced, not forced
—he fancies he wants a reason for everything, though *inter nos* he is too illogical to
be able clearly to sift error from truth—
hence the self-abnegation with which he
has listened to Lently—till yesterday, when
self-will asserted itself in opposition to the
dogmas of his party; and the strife has
filled his mind with rebellion.'

'How do you know all this? Did he tell
you?'

'Had he sufficient confidence in me to
make me his confessor, diplomacy would be
unnecessary—no, I have but observed external signs; but I feel quite certain I have
judged aright.'

'Shall we send him off abroad at once?'

'There is no motive,' answered Mr Sivewright, 'he would regard it as simply done
to alienate him from Claire, and would *poser*
for a martyr during his entire absence, and
come back more determined than ever to

have his own way, whatever that way may be ; for, mark me, I don't believe at this moment he has quite made up his mind what it is that he does want.'

' Well, then, you suggest—'

' That contradiction should be carefully and steadily avoided—that he should be allowed to follow the unbiassed dictates of his own feelings.'

' But, my dear Mr Sivewright, where will they lead him ? '

' Into a direct path, I hope, if we guide his steps without his knowing it.   To enable him to fulfil his destinies in life as a younger son, and to marry Miss Bailey with any honour to himself, it is necessary that he should continue his studies ; that long illness of his has been a sad drawback, happening as it did at the beginning of a young man's educational career.   All this should be represented to him clearly and forcibly, and the *modus operandi* practically set forth.'

'Just so—there is the difficulty—where can we send him? He can't go back to Oxford, that you know; he has failed so persistently in his examinations. Oh! Matthew is a terrible thorn—if he were only more like George.'

'I doubt if George would be more successful if he were in Matthew's place—he is an elder son, and is not expected to work; but to return to the case in point. I suggest that for a time Matthew should pursue a course of private study under efficient training—not in ecclesiastical matters, but in classical lore, with a man who will not attempt in any way to interfere with his religious opinions.'

'What a difficult plan—such a man will be quite impossible to find—people are so fond of airing the quirks and ideas they call religion.'

'Just so—still there is an old college friend of mine, who, if he could be induced to charge himself with Matthew for a time, would, I think, prove a valuable mentor. You have seen him, I believe; he was staying with me a few months since.'

'Mr Wharton! why, he is a free-thinker. Oh! Mr Sivewright, we must be careful what we do.'

'Wharton is no more of a free-thinker than I am; he believes in the broad doctrines of Christianity as they are revealed to a clear, capable mind, unclogged by dogma and superstition. He is not a Lently, if that be what you mean; but I fancied we had agreed to give Matthew free agency of thought, and let him find out for himself what he does and does not believe. I am sure he does not know at this moment.'

'Where does Mr Wharton live?' asked Mrs Desborough meekly—she was always more or less awed when the Rev. Lawrence grew positive.

'He lives in London.'

She gave a little start—he perceived it, and went on,—

'Of course I do not dictate that this step should be taken—I only advise. According to my view of the case, there is no more desirable place than London to which we could send Matthew. He will there mix with a set of people as yet quite unknown to him—people who have had their ideas enlarged, their thoughts matured by friction. He will hear opinions asserted, doctrines circulated, which have found no place in his hitherto prescribed orbit. He will pass so rapidly from fresh scene to fresh scene that it will be strange if, in a short time, he has not forgotten to tighten the knot which now binds him to Swanover Cottage and Ravensholme Vicarage; in a word, it seems to me that the chance is so in favour of his becoming a free man under these circumstances, that the experiment is worth the trial—of course, it remains with you and Mr

Desborough to take the subject into earnest and affectionate consideration.'

'To send a young man to London is a bold step,' said Mrs Desborough; 'there are so many temptations.'

'Certainly there are—but under Wharton's guidance, and with the many friends you have, and who will, of course, be civil to Matthew, I have no apprehension of evil— unless a general enlargement of ideas, an expansion of brain capabilities, be considered an evil—which I deny.'

'Of course—of course—ah! if the scheme you propose be certain to make Matthew less of a visionary, and give him the power of thinking boldly and seriously—how gladly would I urge Mr Desborough to adopt it— only, even then, I have scruples. Do you think, my dear Mr Sivewright, that, our object attained, we shall see Matthew a happier man? Have we any right to wrest

from him the perfect faith he has now—and
to give him—what?'

'Truth!' answered the vicar promptly.
'You are mistaken in imagining that Matthew has perfect faith; his mind oscillates
from one chimera to another, till it is choked
with fanaticism—there is no opportunity for
honest growth. Let him see, hear, argue,
feel for himself; and then, if he prefer Lently
and his school to the wider range of views
which have been offered, let him rest peace-
fully in his perfect faith. We shall have
done our duty, which we certainly shall not
be doing if we allow Matthew to grope blind-
folded along luminous pathways, without attempting to remove the bandage.'

Mrs Desborough did not look altogether
satisfied—she was evidently a little bit afraid
of the step recommended by the vicar.
Expanded, though her views had become,
principally from his teaching, still she could
not thoroughly divest herself of the fear all

women have of taking the initiative in a bold venture; besides, there were times when Mrs Desborough herself was under the influence of Mr Lently's fervid preaching, and perhaps—had she not been personally attracted to Mr Sivewright—it is not wholly improbable that she would have joined the phalanx who had elected Lently to be their Pope.

In women's religion, unfortunately, there is generally mixed a strong amount of hero-worship—and Mrs Desborough was no exception. Many a daring thought or axiom she accepted as uncontrovertible, because it was believed by her dear friend and ally, the Rev. Lawrence Sivewright. As it had been on previous occasions, so it was likely to prove now. Mr Sivewright had thought fit to interfere in the direction of the home affairs at Vantage Park, and he was to obtain —what, by the way, he never doubted—his own way.

No more stern denunciator of priest-craft than the Rev. Lawrence; yet no one more ready to make use of the power he managed to hold through his office—call him moral teacher, or any other latitudinarian name he might elect.

While Mrs Desborough thought, he walked silently up and down the room; after he had taken several turns, he stopped in front of her.

'I am rejoiced, my dear friend, to note that you are thinking the matter out in all its bearings before giving a definite opinion. Nothing is so pleasing to a man of my nerve as the exercise of free unbiassed thought; if you differ from me—as you may—what matter? our bond of unity will only be strengthened by argument — nothing so nauseating as perpetual agreement between friends.'

'But I am afraid we shall not have the pleasure of a quarrel this morning. I am beginning to think you are right—as you invariably are—this is the best, in fact the only plan that will save Matthew.' Mrs Desborough held out her hand to the vicar, who pressed it warmly.

So the issue of Matthew's life having been weighed in the scales of Mrs Desborough and Mr Sivewright's philosophy, it was decided that—the squire's assent, of which they did not doubt, having been obtained—the plan of action they had decided to adopt should be put into force at once, and the lever applied to the machinery which was to have the twofold power of wresting Matthew from his director and his lady-love.

CHAPTER VIII.

A FRESH EXPERIENCE.

ARKET day at Hurton, invariably
a busy time in the usually dull
old country town, with its grey
Bath-stone houses and half-awakened inhabitants! By some established custom,
however, everybody goes to Hurton on
market day, not only the portion of the
community directly responsible for provid-
ing the necessary commodities of life, but
county people; the gentlemen under the
pretext of being really interested in the
prices of animal and vegetable products,
the ladies to shop or flirt.

On a particular Thursday, however, to-

wards the middle of October, at about eleven
o'clock in the day, only *boná fide* buyers and
sellers are to be seen, discussing samples of
corn, the weight and size of pigs and sheep,
the excellence of cheeses and the like. As
by magic, nearly all the idlers have disap-
peared, and it is in vain that the most
eloquent of Cheap Jacks discourses extra-
vagantly on his wares. He can command
but so small a knot of listeners, that he
packs up his boxes of bargains for another
occasion, and gets into the gay yellow gig,
wheels picked out red, which, with the
boxes shining underneath, serves in the
double capacity of advertisement and cart.
Behind this tiny conveyance, which is only
wide enough to hold one person, stands
the smallest of tigers in the most theatrical
of liveries, his occupation being that of
horn blower. A cracked instrument, emit-
ting sounds between a trumpet and a penny
whistle, being used to announce the arrival

of his master's well-known equipage whenever they drive into any of the towns of
which they make the circuit on market
days. Cheap Jack and his miniature domestic are, however, on this occasion, bent
on following in the wake of the rest of
Hurton, for they have no sooner got outside
the town than they turn from the main
road into a narrow lane already thronged
with people of every age and grade.

A balloon is going up from Farmer
Nesbitt's ten-acre piece, and all the popu-
lation of Hurton has flocked to see it. In
the centre of the field lies the huge Levia-
than of the sky, which, in the course of
time, is to be propelled into mid-air, and
the gaping open-mouthed crowd looks on
and wonders from a little distance, the
space enclosed in proximity to the object
of their curious speculation being roped off
for the reception of those individuals whom
our friend, the Cheap Jack, in his inflated

language invariably designates as 'castled swells.'

Foremost among this party—now handling the ropes, now asking pertinaciously leading questions of Mr Garsden, the owner of the balloon—is George Desborough.   Without being very clever or very well read, George has a good deal of general knowledge, picked up chiefly by *viva voce* inquiry, which he maintains is less strain on the mental faculties and more amusing than book learning, while it is the most practical mode of attaining information, because usually accompanied by ocular demonstration.   To judge from the thoroughly interested expression of his face, he is putting his pet theory into practice at this moment ; for so absorbed is he in Mr Garsden's explanations that he utterly fails to perceive that another person is listening with as much interest as himself to the marvellous tales Mr Garsden is relating of the action of machinery and the power of gas. It is not till a voice says close to him, ' I will go up in that balloon. I am resolved. Will you take me, Mr Garsden, for five pounds ? I'll risk my neck with pleasure,' that George Desborough looks round and lifts his hat with a smile to Mrs Tremayne.

'Brave—I know you are,' he observes gallantly. ' But, of course, you do not mean in sober earnest that you will go up in that thing ?'

'I never say what I don't mean,' answered Violet laughing, 'a fact which you will discover when you know me better. I am going up in that balloon ; there would be no fun if there were no danger.'

' But the duchess !' and George looked round.

' The duchess is not here, the duke would not let her come, he thought it *infra dig.* or some nonsense ; but no one has any right to control me, thank goodness.'

'Is it such a happy thing to stand all alone in the world?' asked George. 'I always thought women liked to have some-one to lean against.'

'Lean against! For one sturdy oak there are a hundred thousand osier twigs to be found. Most of my male acquaint-ances belong to the last-named species, so I am learning to pick my own steps with-out support; and by way of proving my strength I am going up in that balloon.'

'If a body will to Cupar, maun to Cupar,' said George, laughingly quoting the old Scotch proverb. 'Still I know no reason why the body maun to Cupar alone. I am quite prepared to go too.'

'You—in that balloon? What would your mother say?'

George grew instantly serious. No man, however he may love his maternal parent, likes to be twitted about the affection.

' My mother is no coward,' he answered ; 'and is fond of new experiences. If she were here I doubt if we should prevent her from accompanying us.'

' That acknowledgment on your part is chaperonage enough for anybody. So arrange with Mr Garsden, and let us rise towards heaven as soon as possible. I doubt if we shall either of us ever have another chance.'

George, taken at his word, complied, and while he was making preliminary arrangements with Mr Garsden, Mistress Violet looked round at the assembled spectators, and rejoiced at the expression of wonder she saw depicted on several faces when it became known that the lady from Montarlis Castle was actually going to trust her life in that ungainly machine. There was, however, no mistake about the matter ; the ducal carriage was waiting for her, and they heard the order given to the ducal servants.

'Go back to Montarlis without me, and tell her grace I shall probably arrive in the balloon. You can put me down on the lawn, can't you, Mr Garsden?'

The aeronaut shook his head.

'That I cannot promise. The route we take must depend entirely on the wind; but I will do my best.'

'All right. I daresay the wind will take us where we want to go, at least we'll hope so. Tell her grace, James, that I shall come in the balloon. There is no other message.'

James touched his hat and smiled. He was evidently more sceptical than Mrs Tremayne about the possibility of controlling at will the capricious upper airs.

'Before the carriage really goes, are you sure you have quite made up your mind that—' said George, beginning another appeal; but it was interrupted by a laughing declaration from the lady that she believed 'he was turning frightened, and if that were the case, she begged he would not risk his precious life on her account—she could very well go by herself.'

What could George do but assure Mr Garsden that they were quite ready when he was prepared to start. They got into the car amid the plaudits of the assembled crowd, which was quite enthusiastic over this exhibition of pluck on the part of the pretty, dainty Violet Tremayne, and loud above them all was heard Cheap Jack's voice, expressing in his vernacular that if ever he had a wife, might he find just such another as that ''ere lady.' In fact, to a woman less accustomed to mix in the varied scenes of life, one who had been more carefully secluded, the present demonstration would have been most repellant, and George Desborough looked at Mrs Tremayne wonderingly, as though he expected she would jump out of the car, grow hysterical, or show in some way her dissatisfaction at being made the centre of attraction to the populace, a position to which ladies of the *grand monde*, as a rule, particularly object. Violet Tremayne, on the contrary, seemed quite in her element, said it was a most delightful piece of excitement, that her pulse had not beaten so fast this many a day, and was evidently thoroughly enjoying herself.

At last the ropes are loosed, and the huge balloon with its precious freight rises with startling rapidity from the ground, and starts up into space. George, if he had told the truth, must have acknowledged that his sensations on finding himself wafted above the 'strong firm earth,' whereon his feet were accustomed to tread, were not of the most pleasurable. He was far from being a coward; had faced danger manfully in many a form; but this frolic he regarded as foolhardy and rash in the extreme. Men, as a rule, only enjoy a daring exploit about which they have, or think they have, some knowledge, and on which they can exercise their power of will or muscular strength. Women, on the contrary, are fearless, and consequently most happy when encountering a danger of which they neither see nor understand the extent. A sense of his own total incapacity was painfully present in George's mind as they pursued their skyward journey, and this, combined as it was with a sickening feeling produced by the rapid and unaccustomed ascent, rendered the air voyage by no means Olympian in its impressions.

It was with some difficulty that he managed to answer with any heartiness Violet's spasmodic bursts of joy—disjointed as they were from the fact that she was perpetually rendered almost breathless by the rapid currents of air which every now and then swept past them. Having risen a considerable distance above the earth's surface—so far indeed that

familiar objects, such as barns and churches,
seemed like mere specks, they came to a
sudden stop, and began to sail before the
wind; but on Mr Garsden's throwing out
some sand-bags—to Violet's intense delight
—they swiftly rose again.

'If it were only not quite so cold it
would be perfect,' she said. 'I am so glad
we came—are not you?'

'I shall be glad we came—when we are
safe at home,' he answered. 'You know I
undertook the expedition solely to please you.'

'How charming to think you are so
anxious to give me pleasure, Mr Desborough,' said Violet, as ingenuously as if
she had been only sixteen, and she dropped
her long lashes, for she had been looking
at him very brightly. 'I hope no evil will
come of it,' she went on in a very sober
voice; 'of course I mean for your sake—
no one troubles about me.'

'Oh, Mrs Tremayne, how can you talk

so. Though osier twigs may bend, they are very difficult to break, and you have at least one osier twig at your service.'

' Ah !' and she gave a little sigh.

The rarefied atmosphere up on high was not conducive to sentiment, and moreover Violet was bitterly cold ; still it occurred to her that it were perhaps worth while to make, if possible, a captive of George. So she resisted the impulse to give way to an immoderate fit of laughter, and sat looking very still and just a little perplexed.

' I hope you are not frightened ?' asked George, after watching her in this new mood for a few minutes.

' Frightened at being in this balloon ? Oh no ! I'm not at all afraid at *that*,' and her voice sank almost into a whisper.

' At what then ?'

' Well, a little at you.'

' At me ! Good gracious ! Why, I came on purpose to protect you.'

'Yes, it was very good of you, but I am afraid foolish on my part. There will be such a talk, and Julia and the duke will be so angry; however, it can't be helped now. Don't look so woe-be-gone, Mr Desborough,' for George was really annoyed by this sudden light she had seen fit to throw on the manner of their upward flight.

'Good intentions,' he murmured to himself, 'the devil always mixes himself up with them. I wish to goodness I had never come to this cursed balloon ascent.'

She did not hear his mutterings, or she would scarcely have been flattered. His regrets were destined, however, to be tripled before the adventure came to an end. Even Violet was beginning to have had enough of the exploit, for wrapping her thin *cachemire* jacket more closely round her, she said, shivering,—

'Don't you think, Mr Garsden, we might

begin to think about arriving on the lawn at Montarlis?' Just before she spoke two more sand-bags had been ejected from the car, and the balloon had risen with a sudden and rapid flight, which delighted the aeronaut, but rendered his companions well-nigh breathless.

'Go down already?' asked Mr Garsden in a surprised tone; 'the air is not nearly thin enough to necessitate a descent.'

'But I am very cold,' said Violet, 'and have fully realised what it is to sit on a damp cloud. If that is the chronic condition of angels, I'll none of them.'

She was feebly attempting to feign a degree of jollity she by no means felt, for pluck was oozing out at every pore; what little she still attempted to retain being merely struggled for, to counterpoise, if possible, George Desborough's expression of utter annoyance and dejection.

'Do you really wish to go back to earth?'

he asked her ; 'because if you do I am sure Mr Garsden will at once direct his balloon into a downward route.'

'Yes, yes. We have done enough to say we have been, and that is as much as one ever wants of a thing. Besides, it is no use to be late for dinner.'

'Late for dinner!' Violet Tremayne had yet to learn that air is not so amenable to the power of man as steam and electricity.

Upon George's interference, however, Mr Garsden opened a valve and allowed a portion of the gas which inflated the balloon to escape. Slowly they descended, but, as it appeared to Violet, much more slantingly than they had risen. In answer to her observation on this subject, she was told by Mr Garsden that the wind had got up, but it would be all right, only they must not attempt to come down too fast. So they pottered along for a while, floating before the wind, as it seemed, on a level range.

'I wonder what the time is?' said Violet, feeling half inclined to cry, and giving a violent tug at her watch. It had stopped at two o'clock, George's some three-quarters later.

'There will evidently be no watches in heaven,' prattled Violet, trying a joke; but George did not laugh, and there was a long silence, during which they described an incalculable journey through space.

'Don't you think it is getting very late?' again asked Violet after a while.

'I fancy so, but I have no idea of the hour; we seem to be so far above the sun that one loses all the signs which form a sort of natural dial,' answered George gravely.

'Well, you are not very encouraging, Mr Desborough, I must say. Can't you look jolly, even if you don't feel so.'

'And you?' he asked with a smile.

'Oh, I am only cold. Mr Garsden, are you ever going to take me home?'

'I hope so, madam; but I am afraid it will not be to-night.'

'Not to-night!' and Violet gave a shriek. 'You don't mean to say I am to sleep in this thing, and have no food! I am starving already, and what will everybody say?'

'I hope we shall have reached comfortable quarters before night,' answered the aeronaut, 'though I am afraid they will not be at Montarlis Castle.'

'What on earth do you mean? Mr Desborough, I must go home.' But George did not answer—he seemed bereft of utterance.

'Can't you speak? Tell me—where are we—why sha'n't I be at Montarlis Castle? Is there any danger?'

'We are crossing the German Ocean,' was George's terse reply.

'Good God!' and Violet looked so wild that he seized her by both hands, fearful lest in her dismay she should throw herself out of the car.

'It is all right—there is no cause for alarm—we shall be in Holland before dark,' said Mr Garsden; 'it is a very good wind, and there is a lovely open space where we can descend not far from the Hague.'

'Holland—the Hague — is it all some horrible dream?' and Violet began to laugh hysterically. 'Why did you bring me, Mr Desborough? It is all your fault; men always want women to do foolish things.'

Poor George, it was rather hard on him to be thus falsely accused; but he did not attempt to vindicate himself, only sought to soothe and tranquillise her. He had promised to see her through this adventure, he said, and cost what it might he would keep his word—at least there should be no scandal. But Violet's nerves having once given way could not be controlled, and for the rest of the dreadful journey she whimpered, sobbed, and asked puerile questions by turns; perhaps George liked her better thus than in her usual dashing, mirthful mood; at all events he was very tender and gentle in his treatment of her. And so minutes grew into hours, and a murky darkness seemed to be stealing all around.

'I am really frightened now,' whispered Violet, almost clinging on to George. He encouraged her by a hand pressure and a few almost loving words. The balloon was descending rapidly—the sea was crossed— the danger was nearly passed, if only there was sufficient light to discern the open space to which Mr Garsden alluded. For half-an-hour the suspense endured by the two unpractised aeronauts seemed like the years of a long protracted agony. At last it was over—they were safe on *terra firma*, and there was just enough light left in the sky to see Violet's white face as she lay in a dead faint in George's arms.

Alone—they two—in the open country some-where between the Hague and Rotterdam.

CHAPTER IX.

'WHERE AM I?'

'WHERE am I? This is not Mont-arlis.' And Violet Tremayne looked round wildly when she found herself in a strange room—an honest-looking Dutch woman leaning over her with as much apprehension on her countenance as though she feared her patient were already dead. But the stamen of life was very strong in Mrs Tremayne, stronger than her slight frame denoted, and having pronounced these words as one waking from a long dream, she sprang from a bed on which she had found herself lying, and stood on the floor confronting her attendant. It was dark, that is to say, the first streaks of early morning were just peeping into the dimly-lighted room, when Violet awoke from the long heavy sleep, which, under the combined influences of strong air and fright, had begun with an unconsciousness which had alarmed both her male companions. She ran her fingers through her crispy curling hair and pondered. The situation was an anomalous one.

Ah! she remembered it all now, and George Desborough—the hero of this mad adventure—where was he?

She asked the question sharply of the woman who stood looking at her with a sort of stupefied air; but no knowledge of English had penetrated into the good Dutch woman's mind, and when, by slow degrees, she had sufficiently recovered from the surprise Violet's sudden resurrection had occasioned, she trotted out of the room. In a few minutes she came back accompanied by a tall thin scraggy female in very light attire, with an old shawl thrown round her shoulders, and her hair scrambled up into a knot at the top of her head. It was obvious she had just got up on being summoned by the attendant, who had been desired to tell her when Violet should awake.

Mrs Tremayne had pulled back the curtains and was looking out of the window; it was just sufficiently light for her to see that she was in a somewhat lonely abode —probably a farm-house, a very flat unpicturesque - looking country being round her, interspersed with numberless small canals; but Violet was in no humour to be impressed by either the beauty or the ugliness of her surroundings — she was thoroughly vexed at the position into which her love of frolic had plunged her. She turned sharply round and asked the new comer tartly,—

'Can no one speak English or French?'

'I can your language a little,' answered Madame Hooght, the proprietress of the house in which Violet found herself.

'That is all right ; then give me something to eat, for I am starving, and tell Mr Desborough to make haste and let us start at once.'

'Your husband, madame, sleeps!' answered the woman shortly.

'Yes—in the churchyard at Hyères!' muttered Violet to herself ; but she did not attempt to rectify the statement, only turned with avidity to some hot milk and farm-house bread which her attendant of the night had just brought into her room. Annoyed as she was at the turn affairs had taken, yet body as usual asserted its dominion over mind, and she hailed the food with a welcome, and ate with as much relish as if the fact of her impromptu visit to Holland left nothing to be desired in its circumstances. Having finished her repast, she plunged her head into

a basin of fresh cold water, and then began
to twist into becoming positions her somewhat rebellious locks—to the no small
surprise of Madame Hooght, who had never
before received into her frugal homestead a
visitor of Violet's type. During these opera-
tions Violet rattled on, receiving, however,
but very doubtful answers to her remarks,
the fact being that Madame Hooght's knowledge of English was too limited for her to
understand the half that was said. Having
brushed, with the assistance of Madame
Hooght, her pretty fawn-coloured autumn
dress, and arranged the red bows as only
such deft fingers as she possessed could have
freshened what, at first sight, seemed disor-
dered tangle, Violet began to wonder when
George would be forthcoming, and what was
the wisest step to take under the difficult circumstances in which she had placed herself.
A little tap at the door, and the hard-featured
Dutch servant entered with a tiny note.

'Breakfast is served in a lower room. Was Mrs Tremayne rested? Would she come down?'

Violet assented at once; an interview with her *cavalier servente* was exactly what she wanted, and in a few minutes she tripped into the homely farm-house parlour with as much self-possession as though it had been the great breakfast-room at Montarlis Castle.

'Good morning, Mr Desborough. I hope you slept well?' and she held out her hand carelessly.

George, however, by no means reflected the lady's buoyancy of greeting.

He held her hand in his for a minute, and then said very gravely,—

'I am so sorry—for you.'

Violet took the cue in a moment; her eyes dropped.

'Ah yes; but it is my own fault; I must suffer for selfishness, you know. Come and have your breakfast, dear Mr Desborough;

do not make yourself unhappy on my account. What has become of Garsden ? I thought I should have found him here.'

' He is looking after his balloon.'

' Horrible invention ballooning. I wish I had never been curious about it,' said Violet with a little shiver.

'Yes, indeed,' and George looked dismally into an egg he had just cracked. 'I am glad you did not catch cold. I was afraid you would be quite ill to-day.'

' Oh, I am pretty well, thank goodness ; but don't you think we had better be getting home ?' and Violet gave him a cup of coffee.

'Yes, I suppose so ; though it is very pleasant here.'

' It might be pleasant enough,' she answered, ' if it were not for a horribly evil-tongued world, which is sure to interfere with every happiness that is not quite conventional. I quite dread to arrive at Mont-arlis. What will the duke say ?'

'You have a home of your own, have you not?' observed George. 'Why not go there?'

'Oh yes, in London. But won't that look exactly as if— Mr Desborough, I will be guided entirely by you—you shall advise. If I had listened to your advice in the beginning, I should not have been in this scrape now—get me out of it,' and she pushed all the cups and plates on one side, and doubling her two arms on the table, she leaned on them and looked into his face.

'There is a boat leaves Rotterdam for Harwich at two o'clock this afternoon. We shall reach London about six o'clock to-morrow morning.'

'Another night away!' and Violet hid her face in her folded arms.

'Shall I go over to England by myself, and send some friend or your maid to fetch you?' suggested George.

'No,' she said, springing up suddenly.

'We have begun the adventure together—
let us finish it. I don't care much what the
world says; there is such a thing as living
down an outcry, I suppose?'

'Mrs Tremayne—Violet — we have met
so seldom that I am afraid you will think
me presuming, but this little adventure has
thrown us together, has it not? Will you
be my wife?'

'Oh, Mr Desborough! it is too bad to
ask me such a question now. If I say
"No," it will make it very awkward for us
to travel home together, and if I say "Yes,"
I am afraid it will make it rather worse,'
and she laughed, more perhaps from excitement than because she saw any fun in
the position of affairs.

'I do not understand,' answered George
soberly; 'as my wife, no one will dare make
any remark about this unfortunate little occurrence, and you will at least be free from
the tongue of scandal.'

'If that is your only reason—merely to shield me from censure—I cannot indeed accept the sacrifice,' and Violet made him a little curtsey.

'My only reason! how can you suspect me of such a thing? Have you not learnt that I love you, sweet Violet? in truth I have done my best to make you understand.'

'Ah!' she said, 'is this so?' and she looked down with the pensive expression to which she had treated him more than once; 'it is a pity, for what are we to do?'

'Tell me first that you reciprocate the feeling just a little, and then I will tell you what we shall do.'

'Well, I don't hate you,' she said laughing, and holding out her hand to him. It was quite impossible for Violet to be sentimental for more than two consecutive minutes.

'And you accept me as a lawful protector?'

' Well, *faute de mieux*—yes.'

' You won't back out when you get to England and are amongst your friends ? ' he asked wistfully, for he was really very much smitten with Violet, and yet did not quite understand her wilful ways and merry badinage.

' Good gracious! no. Why should I? You are better than most of the osier twigs—in fact, I am not sure you are one at all. Under my training you might even turn out an elm or an oak ; but I'll only consent to this little arrangement between us on one condition.'

' Name it. Whatever it is—I accede.'

' Dear me, how accommodating you are now. After a year of marriage won't the tables be turned. Remember I am a widow, Mr Desborough. I know all the weak places.'

' Never mind, as long as past experience does not prevent you from trying the experiment again. What are the terms ? '

'That until this day six months no one is to know one word about the conversation that has passed between us to-day.'

'And wherefore?'

'To save my reputation of course. As long as the world thinks we are mere ordinary acquaintances, no one will trouble to talk about us; the moment they think we are lovers there will be a fine tale. Don't you see?'

'Well, not exactly,' answered George; 'surely as my wife you would be safe from all slander?'

'Yes—then, but not now. I tell you no one must know of this rapid engagement— not even dear Julia or your mother. It must grow—believe me it must grow. Cesar's wife must not be suspected, they say, and I'm afraid if we are not very careful Cesar's *fiancée* will come in for a very large share of suspicion.'

'Are—are we not to meet and see each

other ? This is a very severe verdict, Violet.'

' Of course we are, at the houses of mutual friends, and the tiny acquaintance sprung up in a balloon will ripen slowly into a life-long love with which no divorce court shall ever interfere. Oh ! it will be so ridiculously respectable, whereas if we were to go back now and proclaim ourselves engaged — heaven, or the other place, only knows what people would say.'

' And in six months you really promise to marry me ? '

' Soon after six months. Yes. I suppose so. You have won me by a *coup de main ;* and now, my lord, perhaps you will have the goodness to woo me.'

' That will be no unpleasing task,' said George, kissing her hand.

' Oh ! not now, we must arrive in England first, and then you shall begin quite *en régle.* The boat does not go till two o'clock.

you say; let us have a look at Rotterdam,
and see if we will choose Holland for our
honeymoon.'

In another half-hour they bade adieu to
Madame Hooght, who was still impressed
with the idea that they were man and wife,
and after a little conversation with Mr Garsden, who was arranging his balloon pre-
paratory to starting off in it with the hope
of reaching England, Mrs Tremayne and
George Desborough set off for Rotterdam.
They arrived in the Hoogstras about eleven
o'clock, having blundered slowly along the
four miles which lay between them and the
town in a heavy ungainly conveyance be-
longing to the proprietress of the farm-
house.

'Let us see it all as we are here, and
leave fretting over circumstances till our
escapade has found us out,' suggested Violet.

So they sauntered along the Boomjes,
Violet for the most part keeping up the

conversational ball, not exactly because she
felt thoroughly happy and at her ease, but
because she was anything but charmed at
the position in which she had placed herself,
and because, above everything, she did not
want George to make love to her. She
liked him quite well enough to marry him—
as an eldest son—but she felt she could
not have love-making added to the excitement under which she was labouring at this
time. If any of his own home circle had
seen George following Mrs Tremayne about
Rotterdam with the sort of faithful servility
usually seen in a dog, they would scarcely
have believed their senses. Only a very
few weeks ago he had smiled derisively at
Matthew's love-lorn condition—could it be
possible that he himself was standing at the
very gate of a fool's paradise, and was going
to allow himself to be led about its bewildering mazes by a woman? No one who had
known George till this moment would credit

it ; the rarefied air up in the altitudes must have affected his whole temperament.

And so they wandered about over the balance bridges, up and down the queer canal-intersected town, looked at Erasmus' statue in the Groote Market ; went into the churches, wondered, speculated, chatted about everything they saw, till at last they found themselves on the quay which stretches into the Maas, and alongside of which was lying the steamer which was to bear them to England.

Of the reception they would meet with on their arrival, perhaps both of them felt a little doubtful—though neither liked to own it to the other.

CHAPTER X.

ANTE-MATRIMONIAL.

THE rage for imitating in the needle-work of to-day the embroidery of the middle ages, has penetrated even into the remote northern counties, and Lady Laura Bailey is sitting working at a frame by the pretty oriel window which has been thrown out to enlarge the sunny morning-room at Swanover Cottage. Art colours, designs from nature lie scattered about—she has studied the whole subject in all its details, patronised and pleaded for every school of work in the kingdom, till some of her friends have been more than a little bored by her pertinacity.

Can it be that her zeal has cooled from the very ardour with which it was at first ignited, for she sits now very thoughtful, one hand leaning idly on the frame, the other toying with a lapful of silk and crewels. Lady Laura, however, is not studying any inartistic flaw which she thinks she has discovered in the design; it is evident that she is dreaming, and no very pleasant dream either, to judge from the pre-occupied expression on her usually sweet, calm face.

Claire—the future of her darling Claire—is the picture she is trying to sketch in her mind at that moment, but she cannot succeed, bright as are the hues in which she begins her painting. Like a dissolving view they pass before she can even retain the fair scene in her memory, and a grey tinted misty foreground enshrouds her sunlit horizon. Matthew has paid almost daily visits to Swanover Cottage ever since that walk he and Claire took through the wood with no chaperone but Prig. He has never breathed a word of his own mental difficulties, or of his mother's objections; but Lady Laura is intuitively sensible that all is not well. She has known Mrs Desborough too long, they have passed together over too many rough bits in life's journey, for her not to be able thoroughly to read the case as it at present stands. Her pride revolts at the idea of Claire marrying a man whose family does not receive her voluntarily; but yet, for Claire, she dreads any contradiction which may bring about a rupture with Matthew. She has already noticed that for the last few days all has not been well with her little girl; that her bright smiles have vanished, her joyous song notes become hushed. She, too, has begun to read the signs, and has not failed to observe that a cloud hangs between her and her lover which she seems powerless to dispel. During the rambles

which they occasionally take in the once
enchanted wood, he wanders on silently by
Claire's side, as it were brooding over some
private wrong; yet no loving questioning on
her part can elicit a satisfactory reply as
to what ails him.

Not surprising then that the mother,
feeling rather than knowing of the existence
of trouble in her daughter's mind, should
let her fingers forget their cunning as her
thoughts wander into her child's misty future.

While she sits pondering there, a footstep is heard on the soft gravel in front
of the cottage. She gathers up the errant
crewels, as though anxious to avoid the
fact of being caught dreaming. It is only
just in time; another second, and the Rev.
Lawrence Sivewright is standing by the
window. Yet Lady Laura is not one of his
fold. Ravensholme is her parish church,
and she attends the Ravensholme services
regularly. She scarcely perhaps follows the

Rev. Luke Lently to the extreme outside boundary of his belief ; but still she receives more comfort from his teaching—it seems something more staple for her womanly clinging nature to rest on than that of Mr Sivewright.

The Vicar of Fernwood-cum-Grasdale is, however, no unwelcome visitor at Swanover Cottage. Lady Laura fully appreciates him as a good companion, though she cannot divest herself of a sense of worldliness, which invariably creeps over her for a while after she has been indulging in a pleasant conversation with Mr Sivewright. On this especial morning she is more than usually glad to see him ; she doubts not he is fully conversant with the subject nearest her heart, and who knows but that he may be able to give her the key for which she has been searching so hopelessly of late. Pushing her embroidery frame into a corner, she goes out into the little vestibule to meet and shake hands with her visitor; the etiquette observed at Vantage Park and Montarlis Castle being seldom practised in the smaller but perhaps more wholesome atmosphere in which Lady Laura dwells.

The first greeting over, and Mr Sivewright seated in the cosy morning-room, he looks round as though in some surprise.

'And Claire—where is Claire?'

'Oh, she is very well. She is out— gone through the wood to take some soup to old Mrs Morris,' and Lady Laura felt the colour rising uncomfortably to her cheeks.

Why had she, truthful and straightforward as she always was, been induced by a sort of instinctive reticence to withhold from Mr Sivewright the fact that Claire had gone out accompanied by Matthew? Whatever her reason, it was a very useless equivocation, as perhaps a faint smile which for a moment played round Mr Sivewright's full lips denoted; but Lady Laura was scarcely clever enough, at all events in that peculiar sort of cleverness, to read his countenance, as Mrs , Desborough would not have failed to do.

'It is very charming to have an only child, and that child a daughter as sweet as Claire,' he observed. 'I always pity people with large families. All the pleasure and interest of watching development of character and noting its lights and shades are lost, from want of time and opportunity, to those parents who are compelled to devote their attention to a crowd of children.'

'Yet one child is a terrible anxiety. The mother who loses her one child is indeed to be pitied, or supposing that one child should make a false start or bad choice in life—'

'Your child, my dear Lady Laura, is, happily, a girl, and one endowed with innocence, simplicity, and good sense. You can scarcely be exposed to this latter trial.

If you had a son you might talk of responsibility and anxiety.'

'Oh, boys can make their own way in the world,' said Lady Laura.

'Ay, if they don't begin with that false start to which you alluded just now. Every one who has sons has worry and annoyance —of that you may be very sure. Even our friends the Desboroughs are not exempt.'

'How so—what has happened ?'

'Well, Matthew's future career is, of course, a great anxiety to his mother, and I am not surprised at it, for I cannot at all chalk out his after life.'

Lady Laura looked truly uncomfortable, and began to ask what Mr Sivewright meant ; but he pretended not to hear her, and went on,—

'Then there is George — that little escapade of his with Mrs Tremayne is not very satisfactory. Now, I like George Desborough far better than Matthew. I

think he is made of better stuff; still, I
must say he has been a fool in this instance.'

'What — what has happened? I have
heard nothing.'

'Not the balloon story?'

'Oh, is that all! I can't see that George
Desborough was to blame. Mrs Tremayne
insisted on going up. I am surprised that
the duchess tolerates that woman—she is
always giving rise to some story or another.
What time did they get back?'

'They never have got back,' laughed Mr
Sivewright. 'That is the comical part of
the situation.'

'Good gracious! but they may be killed.'

'Oh dear, no! they are not dead, only
missing. Have you not seen Matthew to-
day?'

'No; I have not.'

Lady Laura had been engaged in some
housekeeping affair when Matthew and

Claire started on their walk. Perhaps she was glad to answer Mr Sivewright's query in the negative, though the fact of its having been put showed that he was by no means ignorant of the existing state of affairs.

'Ah! I imagined you knew all about it, or I should not have mentioned the subject. Gossip is not a commodity in which I usually care to traffic.'

Mr Sivewright perhaps at the moment forgot that a racy story, even if merging on the confines of scandal, was not, as a rule, an unacceptable pleasure to his reverence.

'But now you have begun the conversation, tell me what has happened.'

'Well, the balloon was carried much farther off than either of the aeronauts intended to go, that is all. The adventure may cost George the penalty of marrying Mrs Tremayne—according to my view, a terrible alternative. He is a foolish fellow —a very foolish fellow.'

'Do you mean that marriage is always a mistake, or only as regards Mrs Tremayne?' asked Lady Laura laughing.

'In this instance, I mean personally, as regards Mrs Tremayne, though I do not think I am a strong believer in connubial bliss. I never advocate young marriages for men.'

'Indeed! Do you not think it often steadies a young man?'

'In a very few instances perhaps it does so, but for the most part, after a fool's paradise has existed for a year or two, a man begins to see what a grievous mistake he has made from the very fact of not knowing his own mind. Both George and Matthew Desborough are unmistakable cases in point—Matthew especially.'

'How so?' and Lady Laura looked a little flustered. She particularly wished to ascertain Mr Sivewright's opinion about Matthew Desborough, but, at the same time, she was quite ready to combat it if it did not coincide entirely with her own; his answer consequently by no means pleased her, for he smiled rather sneeringly.

'Knowing Matthew Desborough as you do, you surely do not give him credit for possessing the capability of forming a judgment, or even, could he do so, for having the stability to maintain it.'

'That is severe censure, Mr Sivewright. I am very fond of Matthew, his is a lovable, kindly nature.'

'Granted—and being so, the more easily led. His mother and I have had much serious talk about Matthew lately. I hope the subject of his future life, as it presents itself to our minds, will not fail to be seen in the same light by you.'

'You know—' and Lady Laura hesitated. Mr Sivewright at once helped her through her difficulty.

'I know everything about Matthew and

Claire's summer's day's love making,' he said, 'they are both babies ; but we, my dear lady, who have felt cold March winds and wintry blasts, must look out for the storms, the advent of which they, in their ignorance and innocence, fail to anticipate.'

'You have come as a deputy from Mrs Desborough to express her disapprobation, and to break off if possible all idea of this match, I presume,' said Lady Laura rather anxiously.

'Had that been the case I should have started by telling you so. Quite the contrary, I have come to make an ally of you, in order to promote the happiness of both these young people. For Claire's sake, as well as his own—forgive me if I speak plainly — it is imperative that every effort should be made to strengthen Matthew's weak, it must be owned, somewhat vacillating character. He has failed at Oxford so often that he cannot return there ; yet, as a younger son, it is necessary that he should have a profession. His health is now so far re-established that there is no farther reason for idleness. It is therefore proposed that he should be placed with a tutor, in order to read hard for the next few months.

' I thought he was reading with Mr Lently ?' observed Lady Laura.

The curl of the Rev. Lawrence's finely chiselled nostril was sufficient reply to show at what a low estimate he held Mr Lently's scholarship.

' He must have regular discipline in matters of study, and unbiassed freedom of thought ; that he can only obtain by having a wider range given to his mental faculties than they can possibly have among their present cramped surroundings. The only chance for Matthew is to leave him for a time entirely unshackled by all engagements. Let him have no church,

no restraints, no opinions for a while. At
the end of six months he will perhaps
have learned to sift the dogmas and doctrines with which his mind is now filled,
and be capable of forming an honest
wholesome judgment.'

'I suppose I am to infer that you wish
him to be equally free in matters connected
with the heart as in those bearing reference
to mind?' said Lady Laura.

'Naturally. If Matthew is to go away
for the next six months to seek truth for
himself, he must do so quite unfettered, or
it is impossible that he will ever find it.'

'It is a dangerous experiment,' observed
the lady thoughtfully.

'It is Matthew's only chance of being a
man instead of a puppet.'

'I do not presume to have your knowledge of character, or Mrs Desborough's
cleverness; but I am sorry—very sorry,'
and Lady Laura sighed.

' I cannot see the efficacy of the plan. If Matthew were my son I should pause for a long while, pray very fervently, before I allowed him to run so frightful a risk.'

' The risk is in his idling here and having his mind continually racked by conflicting opinions with which he is incapable of grappling, much less of classifying them.'

' Does he know of this change in his life ? Has he consented to make the trial ? '

' Since he has quarrelled with Lently, he is, I fancy, only too thankful to find a new prop.'

' Quarrelled with Mr Lently ?   I had no idea of this. What has the quarrel been about ? '

' It seems that it is a matter of conscience with Lently, that clergy should not marry.'

' Ah !' and Lady Laura looked very careworn and anxious.   ' This then is the reason that Matthew seems so out of spirits, while

Claire looks wonderingly at the change in him.'

'It is impossible for Matthew either to find happiness himself or to afford it to Claire in the existing position of affairs. Now, my dear Lady Laura, do you see how imperative it is that Matthew should learn to think and act for himself?'

'Yes, yes. Of course he should do that; but still he wants guidance.'

'He has been in leading strings too long. Mr Wharton, a scholarly friend of mine, to whom his father has decided on sending him, will of course watch for stumbles on the road to truth, but Matthew must learn to traverse it alone. He goes up to town next week, I believe.'

All this intelligence fell like a thunderbolt on Lady Laura. As she said, she was not clever, but she was a good, simplehearted, loving woman, whose faith in holy things was strong, and whose way without it would have been very blank and desolate. Mrs Desborough and Mr Sivewright's bolder opinions gave her no desire to entertain them—the very self-reliance they imposed, would have been irksome to her. According to her idea, Matthew would be safer and happier, living on in blind belief, than having his eyes opened to broader, wider views; yet what could she do to prevent the experiment his mother and her spiritual director were bent on trying? She could but pray for the boy she loved well enough to entrust with the future welfare of her Claire. Her eyes filled with tears, as, at this moment, she saw the two young people coming back from their walk in the wood, and she thought of the storm clouds that were gradually rising over the sun of their lives, but of which they were, as yet, only beginning to feel the chilling approach.

The vicar followed the direction of her glance, and smiled as he too saw the young people coming towards the house. He did not attempt to take a hasty departure, but waited quietly till they came in, receiving them with that unctuous paternal patronage, which set them both quite at their ease—only on Lady Laura's brow the thoughtful pre-occupied expression failed to subside.

CHAPTER XI.

CHEAP JACK.

'THEY say—what do they say? Who cares what they say?'

Still for all that Mrs Tremayne looks a trifle graver than is her wont, and wonders for a moment whether she can thoroughly afford to commit a conventional barbarism! Then she bursts out laughing, as her sense of the comic becomes thoroughly awakened, and the Babel of tongues set wagging in scandalous chorus at her expense seems to echo all around her.

Finally, she settles herself in an armchair by the wood fire she had had lighted, the evening being chilly, in the pretty drawing-room in what she affects to call her toy-house in Mayfair, and she proceeds to think. Violet Tremayne is one of those individuals not uncommonly found in society, who act first and think afterwards : hence the numberless scrapes in which she perpetually finds herself involved, and the consequent extravagant expenditure of wits in order to rehabilitate her occasionally dubious position.

Not even experience had taught Mrs Tremayne prudence, and goodness knows she had had a more violent tussle with the ups and downs of life than is the usual lot of women. Perhaps vicissitude to her was like alcohol to the drunkard, a stimulant without which existence would be intolerable, for she never failed to seek adventure, and more or less to rejoice over the imbroglios and difficulties into which her dangerous and somewhat sporting pastimes led her. To her starting

point in life's highway she never alluded,—
evidently the road all about it was too
muddy for her to wish even to return thither.

She had no relations, she was wont to
observe, and if she had, they were people
she did not care to recognise. At seven-
teen she had married Gerald Tremayne,
not because she loved him, but because by
doing so she had helped herself out of the
mud on to a very fair piece of dry ground ;
for Gerald Tremayne, though a gambler
and a *roué*, came of a good old stock, and
had, moreover, large expectations from a
maiden aunt, who gave him credit for an
amount of virtue and sanctity which all his
familiars knew to be non-existent. He
died, however, before his believing relative,
and as the good old lady did not by any
means include his rattling widow in the
belief she had in Gerald, she made a fresh
will, and left her entire property to a
fifteenth cousin.

How Mrs Tremayne ever managed to keep up her tiny establishment in Mayfair no one knew. Sometimes she spent long months at Montarlis, but when she was at home everything was perfectly done, and the appointments almost luxurious. Some said she played high, and that when she was more than usually hospitable and extravagant, a recent visit to Monaco had provided the seeming abundance of money.

Be it as it may, Violet Tremayne has scarcely ever been in a more impecunious position than when she sits in front of the fire on that particular evening, reviewing her past escapade, with a letter just received from George Desborough lying unopened in her lap. She dares not go back to Montarlis, for fear—not of the talk—no amount of chatter would disturb her—she would have an answer for every sally; but for fear of the ominous silence with which she might be received.

She turns the letter over once or twice, sees the Hurton post-mark, but does not open it, only goes off into a dream once more, and wonders whether the Cheap Jack who was so prominently present on the eventful morning of the balloon ascent has made any observation anent her non-appearance. Why should she think of Cheap Jack at that moment — what affinity can he possibly have with the perplexing issues of her life?

Strange—how even at the most serious moments—moments of graver importance than the present to Mrs Tremayne, that capricious and uncontrollable power thought should frequently wander to certain minute frivolous incidents which will, impertinently obtrude themselves on the consideration of the more serious matter one ought to have in mind.

At last having settled her skirts and her ideas to her satisfaction, she runs a mother-of-pearl paper knife daintily along the envelope and draws out George's letter.

' Dearest Violet '—she drops the missive once more in her lap and recommences the thinking process. What right has he to accost her thus—does their compact warrant it ?

Then comes the next query—Does she love George Desborough ?

' No, no,' she answers, with a decided shake of her little head—her pulses beat no higher at the mention of his name, her colour neither comes nor goes as she sees his writing on the sheet of note paper in front of her ; but he is an eldest son—this time the settlements must be quite *en régle*—Violet will not again put her head into the noose without having these arrangements fully carried out. This fact being decided, she turns once more to the missive, and her brow lowers ominously as she reads,—

' Mr Sivewright !'—how dare he interfere

in her affairs? Then *guerre à outrance* is
declared between them—it remains to be
proved which has the greater influence over
the duchess—a little pressure and the whole
thing will right itself. 'I believe I was a
fool not to go straight back to Montarlis
Castle, but it is of no use deceiving myself
—I am just a little bit afraid of the duke;'
and she jumps up and begins to walk about
the tiny room, as though her pent-up feelings seek a wider range. 'And Julia has
not written one word—of course that is
the Rev. Lawrence's fault—really her grace
must be most terribly forgetful if she
imagines she can so easily disembarrass
herself of me. I'll wait two more days, and
then if she does not write or take some
notice, I'll send a telegram, which will, I
think, bring the colour into your aristocratic
cheeks, my grand, white skinned Julia. Yes,
there is a double advantage in going the pace,
for while it warms one's blood at the time,

it also gives one, later on, the power to remind a comrade how near they were to you in the race. They don't love me at Montarlis, but they will have to put up with me till I have either married George Desborough, or some one more advantageous,' and she stood before a mirror in an old venetian frame, and coquettishly arranged her curls.

The visitor's bell startled her.

' Who on earth can it be ? London is at zero, and it is horribly late ! '

She looks at the old clock on the mantelpiece—a quarter to nine. She thrusts George Desborough's letter into her pocket and takes up the third volume of a novel. The button boy, who is Mrs Tremayne's sole male attendant, throws open the door, and presents a card on a silver salver.

' Mr Varley. I don't know the name, it must be some mistake,' says Violet, after a moment's pause, during which a very astute observer might remark that her brow puckers into something very much like a frown.

' What is he like ? '

' Not a gentleman, though his clothes are good,' answers the page, with that promptitude for sorting gold from dross so peculiar to the sharp Londoner.

' Go and ask him his business, Tom,' and during the short absence of the boy, Violet fidgets restlessly about the room. It is obvious she is not quite happy in her mind about the requirements of this unknown Mr Varley.

' Bah ! he is only some horrible dun,' she decides at last, as she throws herself once more in her arm-chair, just as Tom comes back with Mr Varley's message. It is in the form of another card, on which is written,—

' Cheap Jack, from Hurton.'

' Good gracious ! how odd,' exclaims Violet. · ' Show him up at once,' and then to herself, while Tom goes to obey her orders, ' How delightful ! just when I was dull and wanted an adventure, too. I wonder what he can possibly want.'

Cheap Jack came into the room by means of three or four glissades, which served to give his body a most obsequious curve. He was a small active man, with sharp features and a hook nose—in fact he was so very much over-nosed that one almost forgot that his face had any other characteristic, though in reality his twinkling eyes revealed latent cleverness. He was evidently got up for the occasion, and had expended much pomatum in plastering his straight black hair close to his cocoanut - shaped head. The blue and white striped blouse, and blue velvet gold-embroidered smoking-cap which he wore when exercising the functions of his calling were replaced by a much creased black .frock-coat, buttoned up in the front, and surmounted by a scarlet cravat tied in an ingeniously intricate bow. He had left his hat in the hall, but he carried in his hand a box about a foot square, which he held up towards Violet as he chassé-ed up to her. She met him with a peal of laughter, but it was so pleasant and cheery that there was nothing to offend him in the sound; on the contrary, it seemed to fall on his ear as a welcome, for he stopped suddenly, and looked up smiling at the laugher.

'It was put up for you in a raffle at Meckham Fair, and won,' he said, putting the box on a table close to Mrs Tremayne.

'What?' she asked, still laughing; but she looked at the box very much askance, as though afraid it might contain some explosive substance.

'Mementoes of great deeds is due to every heroine,' explained Mr Varley pomp- .

ously, with strong accents on all the wrong syllables.

' I don't in the least understand—you have made some egregious mistake.'

' Mistake, madam. I have been in the cheap line too long to make many mistakes. Open that there box, if you please. Don't be afraid, it ain't nothing as 'ull jump,' for he could not help remarking a certain amount of nervous trepidation in Violet's manner.

With dainty manipulation, and standing as far off from the box as she possibly could, she cut the string, and then jerked open the lid with the point of her knife. Nothing but a mass of paper and shavings lay before her.

' I have opened the box, please take out the paper,' she said, looking a little beseechingly at Cheap Jack, and moving to a still more respectful distance from the table. He observed her with a smile, and having removed a deep layer of shavings, displayed a glass balloon of tiny dimensions. Violet gave a little scream.

'You nasty rude man, who sent you here to twit me? Take away your horrid toy, and never let me see your face again.'

Cheap Jack's countenance fell to zero. This was by no means the reception on which he had calculated when the admiration Mrs Tremayne's daring exploit had awakened in him prompted him to present her with the fairy balloon which, chance having placed it in his hands, he thought was a fitting memento, as he called it, of a great occasion. But how could Cheap Jack know that Violet deeply regretted the adventure, and would fain have its very remembrance obliterated for ever from the mind of man and woman? How could he tell that she was at that moment depressed by the ominous stillness which, reigning among her friends, made her dread the bursting of a storm which should carry her away from her place in society by its up-rooting violence.

They looked at each other for a few seconds, these two anomalous subjects, and each tried to take stock of the other's feelings. From Mr Varley's pained, humiliated expression Violet inferred that he was a principal and not an agent, and by the sudden jumping at a conclusion for which she was celebrated, she resolved to use him if possible to her advantage; while he—well, he was accustomed to snubs, yet he regretted just a little bit that he had come—that, carried away by his great admiration for Mrs Tremayne, he had so far forgotten himself as to be guilty of a piece of unwarrantable presumption. When the short watch they had both been keeping over each other's features was over, Mr Varley began to cover up his bit of glass work, while Violet was the first to speak.

'Stop a minute,' she said, 'let me look at it just once again.'

He took it out of the box and held it up in all its dainty beauty.

'It's first rate workmanship—blown at the best manufactory in England, every detail perfect, even to cords.'

'Ah! I wish I had never seen a machine like that before, Mr—' and Violet looked at the card lying on the table before she ventured on the word, '"Varley."'

'Wasn't your experience a pleasant one? I am sorry now, you was so brave.'

'And I am to keep this lovely miniature balloon as a trophy or memento, or whatever you call it?' she said laughing, and taking it into her own delicate fingers.

He bowed assent, looking perhaps more surprised than pleased; the sudden change in her manner puzzled this man, who was totally unaccustomed to the vagaries of great ladies. As for *arrière pensée*, it did not

occur to him that such a thing could exist
in this class of life, though he was fully and
entirely alive to the commerce of motive
and cause, which was very briskly proceeded
with in his own trading career.

Mrs Tremayne's next question after she
had delivered herself of a profuse amount
of thanks, produced no especial meaning
to his mind. Merely as something to say
did he regard the query as to when he
was likely to be in the neighbourhood of
Hurton.

'Very soon,' he answered promptly; 'there
is Meckleton Races next week, the course
is just a mile from Vantage Park, Squire
Desborough's place, you know.'

Violet bowed her head.

'I wonder if you would charge yourself
with a commission for me when you go
back into those parts.'

'Would I? why, with all the pleasure in
the world.'

'When can you make it convenient to call here again?'

'Whenever your ladyship pleases to appoint,' Violet had risen to ladyship, as Mr Varley's good-humour increased.

'To-morrow, rather earlier than this, say six o'clock.'

He bowed his head and shuffled his feet as though the carpet were red hot.

'It is only a small parcel I want to send to some one in that neighbourhood, and I shall feel obliged if you will deliver it yourself,' explained Violet, turning the glass balloon round and round with admiring scrutiny, and finally tying it with crimson ribbon to a bracket near the fireplace, while Mr Varley, having promised to deliver the parcel, looked and wondered. Then she rang for the button boy, and bade him bring some glasses and sherry, and having stood with surpassing fortitude the drinking of her own health by her strange guest, she at last succeeded in dismissing him in the happiest frame of mind. He had quite forgotten the snub with which the interview had commenced, and went whistling down the street, looking so universally delighted with himself and the whole world as to make the young and ragged sweeper at the corner observe to a companion,—

'That master had come out of yon house uncommon squiffy.'

Violet laughed. She touched her new toy and set it swinging, and then she stood looking at it and laughed again; finally, having felt that George Desborough's letter was safe in her pocket, she began to turn out the contents of some drawers at the side of a Davenport which had been pushed into a corner, as being neither old enough nor new enough for fashion's requirements in the way of furniture.

CHAPTER XII.

MRS GILES.

THE Rev. Luke Lently is standing at his study door—the usual look of stereotyped asceticism seems temporarily to have departed from his face, on which lingers just half a smile. He is rubbing his thin hands slowly together and listening. His companion is a lady long past even the suspicion of loitering within the very elastic boundary known as middle age. She is a dry shrivelled woman with frizzly grey hair which lies in little tufts about her forehead, surmounting a countenance, of which the leading characteristic is asperity. Her clothes, though neat and tidy, have no pretence of being fashionable ; on the contrary, they are ludicrously the reverse, unless very full short skirts, displaying sturdy feet, cased in strong country-made leather boots, may be considered fashionable. Yet this is Mr Lently's pet parishioner—his factotum —the one individual who shares in their fullest degree his beliefs and opinions, and who seeks moreover to assist him in carrying out to the very letter all the multitudinous projects by which he hopes and believes he will coerce mankind into a full participation in all his views.

Mrs Giles has been a widow for fifty years—for the last twenty she has lived what she herself calls 'on the confines of the church,' that is, when translated into plain language, she has been slave to some pet minister, and thus obtained that stimulus in life which she failed to find in the monotony of her childless companionless home. For the first ten years she had served in evangelical leading strings, then she met

Mr Lently, and becoming a convert to his fervid teaching, she had declared herself a zealous disciple ; and when the Rev. Luke gave up a surburban curacy for the more comfortable and remunerative position of Vicar of Ravensholme, Mrs Giles took a cottage in the parish and practised good works under his fatherly supervision. With Mrs Lently she had but little in common ; her existence she designated as the one blot on a good man's life, and her shortcomings were regarded by the rigid practical Mrs Giles with—regretfully be it spoken—a mere modicum of Christian charity. Had she been less severe in her strictures on poor Mr Lently's failings ; had she elected to help and advise the wife, instead of living in a state of flattering subserviency to the husband, who shall say how different might have been the tone of domestic life at Ravensholme ; but Mrs Giles' ideas on the subject of good works did not drift in this direction ; after all, we can only see good or evil according to the light given us.

The Rev. Luke smiles as he listens to Mrs Giles' conversation. It is of mundane affairs. She is administering a little of the luscious jam without which it were impossible to swallow the bitter life pills he daily imposes on himself with conscientious compulsion. The doings at Montarlis Castle and Vantage Park form the staple subject for their talk on these occasions. Strange that human nature, even when purified to the very highest degree, must at times find a valve for its superfluous frailty, and that in cases where greater sins are banished, yet gossip and scandal invariably hold their ground.

The balloon ascent! Yes, Violet Tremayne was right—it was the universal topic, discoursed of throughout the whole country; no two people met without throwing a stone at the glass house in which she and George Desborough had rashly located themselves;

even Mrs Giles and Mr Lently gave way to
unkindly allusions and little jokes ; but then,
be it remembered, Mr Lently was never permitted to cross the threshold of Montarlis
Castle, and felt that he was only received on
sufferance at Vantage Park.   Moreover, he
had not afforded himself the luxury of treat-
ing those opposed to him in matters of faith
with indifference, as Mr Sivewright did.   He
never forgave a snub, though he frequently
exposed himself to the reception of one, not
having neglected to court more than one from
the Duke of Montarlis, to whom he was perfectly aware that his particular tenets were
especially distasteful.

He smiled at the fancy of the airy equipage bearing the dashing Mrs Tremayne
into the realms of space, it was a freak of
the elements which could not avoid awaking
a smile ; but the passing mirthful ebullition
died on a sudden to be replaced by a stern,
cold glance at Mrs Giles' next remark.

'And now Mr George Desborough will have to marry the dainty lady. To finish the pretty romance, there will be two Desborough marriages, for they say Matthew is engaged to Miss Bailey.'

'God forbid!' ejaculated the Rev. Luke fervidly. 'I have placed my veto on the unholy step.'

'And has Matthew promised to be obedient? Alas! my dear pastor, I fear there is more mischief going on in the fold than you are aware of.'

Mrs Giles, in her love of gossip, could not even resist giving information which she knew would wound instead of amuse her beloved vicar.

'How so, what fresh calamity has fallen on my flock?'

'Only that you are soon to lose one of them altogether.'

'Indeed, what have you heard?'

'That Matthew is going to be sent to a tutor in London.'

'A wise measure — a very wise measure!' half soliloquised Lently, 'that is if the choice has fallen on a just and faithful man.'

'Some years ago, when I was a much younger woman than I am now, and consequently more given to the vanities of the world, I was living in the neighbourhood of London ; next door to my dwelling there resided in a state of semi-genteel poverty a family of the name of Wharton. They held their heads up pretty high, notwithstanding their want of means, for they were born among the aristocracy—at least she was— the husband was a literary man — spent his time among old folios and philosophical treatises. Mrs Wharton and the girls were musical, however, and I have spent more than one evening pleasantly enough in their society.'

' Why are you telling me this now ? ' interrupted her companion.

' You will see the point directly if you will
only have a due amount of patience, Mr
Lently. After I had known the family about
six months a son appeared, of whom till then
I had only heard. He had been abroad
finishing his education, in other words, cram-
ming his head with metaphysical German
nonsense, and losing what small amount of
religious faith he may ever have possessed.
I thought him a fine young fellow in those
days,—thanks to your teaching, I regard him
as a heathen now. Dear me ! I daresay he is
a man of fifty by this time. He was a very—
permit me the word—jolly sort of young man,
strong in his own opinions, eloquent in his
talk—almost converted me into the belief
that free thought was the only aim and
object of man. He was little more than a
boy then—he is a professor now, with no
end of letters strung after his name, and

he it is who has been selected as Matthew's tutor.'

A low moan of agony escaped from Mr Lently's lips, his tight Roman collar evidently choked him—and then he asked with sudden energy, as though hope, half crushed by Mrs Giles' intelligence, had sprung once more into life.

' But he, like yourself, has been converted, has given up these pernicious opinions long since ? '

She shook her head.

' Though he is professedly a scholar, he is grovelling in the pathways of darkness,' she answered, and then they both sighed in chorus, and Lently asked,—

' Who has done this evil thing ? '

' Mr Wharton is an intimate friend of the Vicar of Fernwood-cum-Grasdale.'

' Sivewright ! He will have much to answer for. How a man dare live in open

defiance of all the canons of holy Church as
he does, is a mystery to me.'

'How odd Matthew should not have told
you of the change in his plans.'

'Matthew is not wholly subjugated. He
is still restive of the yoke. He cannot give
himself up soul and body to authority. I
have yet much vacillation of purpose to fear
for Matthew. The idea that he has thought
of entering on the matrimonial state fills my
mind with sadness.'

'Gracious!' ejaculated Mrs Giles, on whose
ear at that moment fell discordant sounds of
nursery tribulation, and before she had time
to transfer her feelings into words, the
younger members of the Lently family ran
shrieking round the corner of the house,
utterly regardless of their father's frowns or
their mother's whining threats, which were
heard in the far distance feebly promising
a punishment she was powerless to inflict.
Mrs Giles, to whom the little Lentlys were

particularly antipathetic—in fact, she always strove in her own mind to ignore the fact that the pastor had any family and belongings—immediately took her leave, walking down the footway into the churchyard, which she crossed, coming into the main road by a little wicket just as Mr Sivewright was rid· ing lazily by on a sleek cob, which was the envy of more than one middle-aged squire. Certainly the Rev. Lawrence Sivewright had the peculiar knack of invariably discovering and possessing himself of the best things in life. He raised his hat with an unctuous bow to Mrs Giles, and went on his way, she looking after him the while with very vinegarish glances. There was a sovereignty of manner about Mr Sivewright, an indifference to their opinions and their dictums, which made all the opposite religious faction fear him.

No surer mode of holding a high position in the eyes of others than to seem to have an exalted place in your own esteem.

That Mr Sivewright acted on this axiom,
either purposely or by accident, there is little
doubt. Mrs Giles' way lay in the same direction as that of the mounted divine, who was
going to Montarlis Castle. She followed
him for a few hundred yards, and then she
turned in at a little green gate. She stood
leaning against the gate looking after him ;
when he was quite out of sight she walked
slowly up a narrow path leading to a cottage,
of which the door stood open, and entering a
small rigidly furnished sitting-room sat down.
She looked round the room with a very self-
satisfied expression in her face—the religious
pictures which were here and there dotted on
the white walls reminded her of various phases
of feeling, under the dominion of which she
had hung them there—the bare floor with its
occasional rug, the high-backed cushionless
chairs, the coverless wooden tables, the cur-
tainless windows, even the mediæval clock
serving for sole mantel-shelf ornamentation

all pointed to a life of asceticism in which Mrs Giles gloried, a life of self-regulated, self-inflicted conventual rule. Whether for the love of God or for the love of the Rev. Luke Lently she had chosen this life, it had been difficult for Mrs Giles herself to have defined, so inseparably did she connect in her mind the zealous friend whose teaching was so dear to her, with the Deity they both served according to their light. Yet Mrs Giles had not always been what she now was — did she not herself tell Mr Lently so but half-an-hour ago. Of all the history of her past life, however, she had not thought it necessary to inform him— as it was enclosed in the almost impervious wrapper of long long ago ; perhaps she had forgotten what lay therein concealed. Either the sight of the Rev. Lawrence Sivewright riding along the road towards Montarlis had re-called it, or perhaps it was the conversation anent Mr Wharton which she had just had with her pastor. Yet what possible connection could or did exist between Mrs Giles' very middle-class career and the previous history of that particularly thorough-bred scholar-like gentleman Mr Sivewright?

Very certain it is that he never bestowed a thought on Mrs Giles, or even mentioned her name when she was alluded to in the neighbourhood, simply connecting her existence with that of Mr Lently, and smiling at what he called 'a flagrant piece of pet parson worship.'

Of course the friendships borne him by the Duchess of Montarlis and Mrs Desborough were individual, between woman and man, and had nothing whatever to do with divine office.

If Mr Sivewright had ever seen Mrs Giles in years gone by, he had entirely forgotten the fact; yet she could have told, had she chosen, more than one episode of his early youth, when he and

young Wharton, after being at Oxford together, had devoted a year to philosophy
in a German university, and had come back
to London to start on their career as men ;
Wharton simply signing himself philosopher,
while Lawrence Sivewright became a clerk
in holy orders, with the Vicarage of Fernwood-cum-Grasdale in prospect.

Mrs Giles sits thinking over all this, and
the tidy little village hand-maiden bringing in
the tea wonders why the mistress, usually so
exact in all the details of daily life, ' daunders '
instead of taking off her bonnet and cape,
as she is wont to do the moment she enters
the house, instantly beginning some active
employment, either in connection with soul
or body.   But even the sight of Patty with
the tea does not move Mrs Giles, and the
girl has placed it on the table and made
a good deal of clatter with plates and knives
before her mistress goes up the little stair-
case to her own room ; and even when she

has reached it, instead of at once replacing her poke bonnet by the white full bordered cap she usually wears, she stands looking out of the window. 'Matthew Desborough' is the name that almost mechanically drops from her lips; then it is not Lawrence Sivewright's past over which she is dreaming? No—only as it bears any influence on Matthew Desborough's present. Not that Mrs Giles has any personal and deep interest in that young man, except as regards his relations with Mr Lently. Perhaps she had rejoiced when she thought he was resolved to waive the question of orders, and was determined to marry Claire Bailey. Not for the Church's sake, be it thoroughly understood; but Mrs Giles was a woman, though an old one, and she was anxious to keep her influence over her pastor fresh and full. The age at which jealousy dies in the feminine heart has never yet been clearly defined.

CHAPTER XIII.

CRACKLING ICE.

 FEW seconds after the Vicar of Fernwood-cum-Grasdale had lifted his hat to Mrs Giles he forgot the fact of her existence; and he and his sleek cob, alike enjoying the beauty of a soft autumnal afternoon, journeyed tranquilly along towards Montarlis Castle, the vicar guessing as little as did his equine companion how many ruminations meeting him had produced in the mind of the 'eccentric widow,' as he usually designated her.

Arrived at his destination, and his cob having been led round to the ducal stables, he was at once ushered into the library, where five o'clock tea had preceded his advent by a few minutes.

If a *tête-à-tête* talk with the duchess was the object of his visit, he was destined to be disappointed, for there was quite a little coterie of privileged intimates sipping the gossip-flavoured beverage, alike welcome in the castle and the cabin.

He shook hands with the fair châtelaine, and bowed to one or two guests but little known to him, while perhaps a very keen observer might have noticed just a tinge of disappointment on his countenance; scarcely, however, because the duchess was surrounded by friends. Mr Sivewright was perfectly aware that it was the usual hour of meeting, and even if he were desirous of a conversation with the duchess, he was fully sensible that under no circumstances is a private talk more thoroughly and conventionally obtained than in a crowd. He only found what he ex-

pected then on entering the richly stored
library at Montarlis Castle, on the many
treasures of which the sun at that moment
was casting, as though lovingly, its depart-
ing rays through the small-paned mullioned
windows—with one exception. There was
a curly-haired brunette seated on a low chair
by the table ; she had thrown a large Gains-
borough hat at her feet, and was doing the
honours of the occasion for the duchess.

'You don't take sugar, I think, Mr Sivewright ? How are you ? ' she said flippantly
with a little nod, holding a large lump
daintily in the tiny old-fashioned tongs as
the vicar approached her.

' Thank you ; no tea.'

Ah ! there was to be found the reason of
Mr Sivewright's disappointed look ; he did
not expect to see Violet Tremayne re-established, at all events not so soon, in her old
familiar relations with the duchess. Further-
more, he had not been consulted on the

matter, which was, at the least, not flattering ;
but he could have passed the seeming neglect
very lightly by, had not the fact of Mrs
Tremayne being there involved, according to
his views, such very grave issues. For a
moment or two the arrival of so important a
member of society as the Vicar of Fernwood
had silenced the busy talkers, all of whom
were ladies, the male guests at Montarlis not
having yet returned from shooting ; but Mr
Sivewright's courteous affable manners soon
set every one chattering again even more
freely than before, and, taking a cup of tea
from Mrs Tremayne, he handed it to the
duchess. Their eyes met in one flash, and
she said very quietly, scarcely moving her
lips as she spoke,—

'I could not help it ;' then as if she feared
even that instantaneous exchange of con-
fidences might be perceived, she went on,—
'Vi, dear, have you forgotten Mrs Belling-
ham ? She has had no tea.'

Meanwhile Mr Sivewright passed to the farther end of the room, with his usual urbanity, to devote himself to a rather pretty-looking shy girl, who was sitting apart from the others. She was only just out, and by no means *au courant* with the dashing talk of the day, having been carefully kept to a school-room routine which admitted no gleams of social light. In her heart she scarcely thanked the vicar for his notice, kind though it seemed, but she hardly knew how, he led the conversation to some of her pet books, and in a very few minutes she was talking glibly, without blushing and paling at every alternate moment. Yet, could she but have known it, she had more to fear from Mr Sivewright than from the usual carpet knights whose platitudes awed her and whose chaff struck terror into her breast.

Mr Sivewright was studying human nature. He was wondering how long it would be

before this frightened child would develop
into the consummate actress most of her
fashionable sisters had become ; and his eye
wandered from the graceful stately duchess,
who was his beau-ideal of womanhood, to the
little rosy beauty with whom he was talking,
and then across the room to the laughing
Violet, till finally he shrugged his shoulders
as though he had come to the conclusion
that women's ways were unguessable riddles,
imposed mercilessly by the gods on men.
At last, so utterly absent did he become,
owing to his mental contemplations, that the
little girl by his side did not fail to remark
it, and extreme shyness being usually the
result of a superabundance of pride, she
felt hurt at his sudden inattention to her
remarks, and starting up, sped briskly across
the room to where her mother was sitting,
and took shelter under her fostering wing.
Mr Sivewright smiled a little sadly ; he was
sorry he had scared the child from his side,

yet he could not resist being amused at the amount of womanliness already developing itself in that young nature—demanding absolute attention and devotion as a right. The vicar sat musing apart from the rest, till Violet Tremayne's gay tones recalled him to the circle round the tea-table, as in bantering accents she exclaimed,—

'Mr Sivewright invariably finds matter wherewith to compose a sermon whenever he comes to Montarlis ; let us have the text of the next homily, reverend sir.'

It was an impertinent challenge under all the circumstances, and Mr Sivewright regarded it as such, and answered promptly,—

> ' Loving goes by haps,
> Some Cupid kills by arrows, some with traps.'

The ready answer occasioned a general laugh, though none perhaps save the duchess and Mrs Tremayne accepted the point.   To the latter it evidently went

straight home, and for a moment or two
paralysed the power of repartee in which
she was usually so strong ; she gave one
searching look at the vicar which revealed
all the deep fund of hatred of which her
heart was capable, and, without even being
a coward, Mr Sivewright might have quailed
before the animosity he had awakened ; but
he remained firm as granite, and gave the
lady look for look, till, recovering her mo-
mentary weakness, she said so gaily and
adroitly as to make him almost like her for
her cleverness,

' Indeed, this is delightful ; let us have a
rehearsal now—tell us all about it, Mr Sivewright—have you been shot or caught, and
by whom ? We thought him invulnerable,
did not we, duchess ? But, after all, he
would not be human if he were without his
Achilles' heel ? '

But the duchess, though appealed to, only
smiled somewhat sadly. She was not pleased

at the fact of being compelled to receive
Violet at Montarlis, not pleased with Mr
Sivewright for calling almost public attention to recent events, and seriously dis-
pleased with circumstances for having pre-
vented her from explaining matters fully to
him she had selected as director and ad-
viser, before this untoward meeting had
occurred. But Violet went on,—

'Now, Mr Sivewright, the sermon, if you
please,' and she pushed a stately old-fashioned
chair towards him, on which she begged him
to be enthroned.

Mr Sivewright declined the seat with a
bow, and with mock gravity quietly placing
himself behind the high chair she had offered,
looked thoroughly *en prône.*

Amusement was depicted on every face,
save that of Violet, who looked defiant,
and the duchess's, who seemed painfully
anxious ; perhaps the vicar felt she might
have trusted him, for though his eye fell

on her lingeringly, he abated no jot of the ceremonial with which he accepted the function imposed on him by Violet; but looking from one to another at the knot of expectant listeners, he began,—

'Spontaneous affection and sheer coercion, these are the two powerful motive forces which actuate the amiable or loving tendencies of man. Happy he or she, as the case may be, on whom the gift of spontaneity is conferred. The lucky individual has but to follow his good impulses and trust faithfully to the blind god who has bestowed them, that he will conduct the suit he himself has instituted to a happy termination with his usual kind supervision. Far be it from us to cavil at or animadvert on godlike agencies. When, too, was Cupid ever known to play false?'

Here the vicar was interrupted by such a chorus of giggles as to stop his interpretations; but not for a moment losing command over his own gravity, when they had somewhat ceased he proceeded,—

'It is, on the contrary, to those who have fallen from their high estate in the love-god's favour that we would address a word of warning and advice. To those who, receiving no impulsive natural affection, elect to seek it at any cost, and erect a temple to Hymen even on the most impossible heights, amid rugged crags and on unculti-vated ground. To such individuals I would paternally say " Beware." A union un-hallowed by Cupid reverts with dismal misery on him who sets the trap—for when was a poor limed bird ever known to submit un-flutteringly to its entanglement; rather does it not take instant flight when the viscous substance by which it has been made cap-tive loses its adhesive qualities. And no glue, believe me, has yet been discovered that is impervious to every vacillating ten-dency of place and time. Stormy days will arrive, tidal waves will overflow the seemingly pleasant river banks ; sooner or later the bird will free himself without Cupid making one single effort to rivet the chain he had no hand in forging. But to illustrate the subject. An instance has lately come to my knowledge which—'

' Really, Mr Sivewright, I cannot see—' It was the duchess who spoke, but Mrs Tremayne stopped her.

' Hush, Julia dear. Let him finish the illustration by all means. Mr Sivewright— the illustration. It will be especially interesting.'

' In a fashionable foreign watering-place, some ten years ago, there was a young girl and a somewhat elderly man she called her father. Theirs was a well-worn tale of gambling, debt, and destitution.'

' Mr Sivewright !'

He paused and looked at Violet Tremayne as she uttered his name in exclamation.

' Did you know this girl, Mrs Tremayne ? '

' I ?   No.   How should I ?   But we scarcely asked for a picture.'

' Still it is a true one.   Shall I finish the sketch ? '

' Yes,' said a chorus of voices, among which the duchess and Mrs Tremayne were alone silent.

He looked at her for a second very pointedly ; then at the duchess, whose countenance still evinced a considerable amount of alarm ; finally he said, as if entirely giving in,—

' I must apologise, ladies, for taking up so much of your time and attention ; really I don't know what excuse I have to offer.'

' You have told us nothing, Mr Sivewright ; but do—' exclaimed a curious old dame.   Violet interrupted her.

' Oh, he knows a set of horrible people ; don't ask him any more,' and she got up from the tea-table.   ' For my part, I think women who set men-traps are fools ; it is against them you were preaching, I believe. There is not a man living that one would not be much better without—your reverence included.'

Everybody laughed a little falsely.

Mr Sivewright's discourse perplexed their minds ; they could not quite see its object, though that it had one, the white face of the duchess too plainly testified. Violet made a diversion, and putting on her hat, said she was going on the terrace to look at the sunset. She was soon followed by the rest of the party, and for a brief space the duchess and Mr Sivewright were left alone.

'How could you walk on crackling ice— for what purpose ?' she asked hurriedly.

'At any cost Mrs Tremayne must no longer be domiciled here. How could you ask her to come back after that balloon business ? I must speak to the duke.'

'My dear friend, you will not—you must not. If you are going to fail me, to whom shall I turn for assistance? I am powerless to coerce Violet Tremayne. She *must* be here, and instead of helping me to stem difficulties, you have made her your mortal enemy. Oh, Mr Sivewright, advise me; what am I to do?'

'I do not understand.'

'Mrs Tremayne holds a secret of mine; unless I keep her in the position of my bosom friend, she will reveal it to my husband.'

'Outwit her by telling him yourself,' said the vicar promptly.

'Oh, I dare not—I dare not. Have not I limed an eagle, and I cannot bear to be cast ignominiously from my eyrie. For mercy's sake, out of friendship to me, leave Violet's affairs alone, and let her arrange them as she will—'

'Let her marry George Desborough, you

mean ; considering my strong personal intimacy with his family, it would scarcely be
a friendly action on my part ; knowing what
I do—'

'Mr Sivewright, I beseech you to be
silent for my sake,' and the duchess's velvety
hand was laid on the vicar's wrist. The
Rev. Lawrence Sivewright was but human ;
notwithstanding his sacred calling, could he
resist this woman's pleading ? He took her
hand in his own, with the air of a man to
whom it was no unusual occurrence, but the
merry troop from the terrace came laughing into the room in total forgetfulness of
the riddle which had been propounded, so
the vicar could not speak. When some half-
hour later he went away, it was with a
graver more thoughtful expression of face
than when Mrs Giles had watched him
leisurely riding up the road.

CHAPTER XIV.

A QUEER BARGAIN.

IT is the morning succeeding the unusually interrupted tea‑chat, when, dressed *à la vivandière* in blue and red flannel, Violet Tremayne is standing alone on the terrace which over‑looks the gardens at Montarlis. She hides her eyes with her hand and looks through the trees, nearly bereft of foliage, as though seeking to distinguish some object in the far distance; with an impatient gesture at its non-appearance she paces rapidly up and down, and then stops to look once more in the same direction. After repeating this manœuvre two or three times, she runs swiftly down the steps at the farther end of the balcony, and crossing the wide lawn without looking round, she speedily disappears from the view of any one who may have been watching her from the windows of the house.

Mrs Tremayne's movements, ever eccentric and erratic, do not as a rule create much observation from those who are accustomed to her habits. They have too frequently investigated some seemingly mysterious doings on her part, to be simply repaid by the information that she had no especial object for her behaviour, to trouble themselves about her goings and comings. Some of her friends had arrived at the conclusion that she was just a little cracked; while the servants and dependants at Montarlis decided that it was 'only Mrs Tremayne's way,' and attached no importance to any unusual circumstance in connection with her. No one guessed that it was part of Violet's plan of life ; she argued that a hundred well acted mysteries, which are no mysteries at all, enable the hundred and first, being a reality, to escape without remark.

The occasion presents itself now, and Violet has judged rightly.

'There goes Mrs Tremayne down into the wood,' the butler remarks to the valet; 'she'll come back at luncheon time with those big pockets full of nuts, and try to persuade every one she has had an adventure;' and so the subject is dropped, while Violet still speeds on, never stopping for a second till she is quite half-a-mile from the house.

This time she has a *bonâ fide* assignation ; and with none other than Mr Varley, the Cheap Jack of Hurton market-place. Violet was too accustomed to utilise the crooked bits and ends of life to let so available an oddity as Mr Varley press himself as it were into her service without retaining him. The heart of man is prone to sudden and wayward likings, and Cheap Jack had formed one of these for Mrs Tremayne, when he saw her for the first time starting on her balloon journey with George Desborough.

'A queer fondness for a unit like me to have for a lady born,' as he himself expressed it; but then he could not guess how much of the gipsy there was in both their natures, producing probably the affinity. It was the first time he had seen Violet since her return to Montarlis, though more than one interview had taken place in London.

'Well, Jack, how are you?'

They had grown quite familiar—that was obvious from Violet's greeting as she approached the large elm close to which Mr Varley was standing. He had left his gay little equipage in the main road, with the tiny tiger in charge, and himself habited in his usual blue blouse and velvet cap was awaiting the lady's arrival.

He pulled his cap off as he heard her voice and made a deep salaam.

He did not seem surprised at her off-handedness—it was a way she had which was so essentially a portion of herself that few people presumed to cavil at it, and assuredly the exception was not likely to be her new acquaintance Mr Varley.

' You executed my commission beautifully,' she said, ' gave my little parcel to the duchess her very own self.'

' Yes, my lady, and a rare bit of luck it was to meet her grace walking alone with the dogs down near the pond yonder.'

' Yes, I know—she told me ; and how did she look when she opened the letter ? '

' Rather skeered like. I was really sorry when I saw it wasn't a pleasant packet.'

' Poor Julia—poor Julia, but she'll get over it, she'll have to bear annoyance like other folk ; you and I don't escape, do we—eh, Jack ? '

Varley shuffled and looked shy, the flattering way in which she seemed to place him on an equality with herself quite overpowered him.

Mrs Tremayne laughed, and asked him what she owed him for all the trouble he had taken ; but the pained expression of the man's face stopped her before she had reached quite the end of her sentence.

' Nothing, my lady—nothing. I am quite repaid by your having granted me the honour of this interview.'

' Good gracious ! Well, you are easily satisfied. I'd come here every day in the week if you would transact all my business for me for that small payment.'

' I am always to command if there is any business to do and I am in these parts ; what's more, I'd stop in these parts if I thought as you wanted me.'

For the first time it occurred to Violet as she looked at him, that she had inspired a

grande passion. She did not flinch from
the idea with repugnance, as it behoved
her position to have done ; alas ! no, she
put it down instantly on her list of con-
quests, feeling a little flattered and very
largely amused. Montarlis was not unfre-
quently dull to one who, like Violet, objected
to the perpetual strictness of high life—here
was a charming valve, by which she might
get rid of any amount of monotony : she
resolved at once to improve the occasion,
and sitting down on the bough of an old
tree which lay on the ground close to her,
she invited Mr Varley to give her some
account of the mode in which he passed
his life. Garrulity was his wonted *forte,*
though he would not have acknowledged
it : but on this occasion Cheap Jack was
a little serious, and consequently inclined
to be silent,—though to most men Violet
Tremayne sitting in a very *degagée* attitude
on the old tree would have been scarcely

an awe-striking picture. She was too impertinent in her ways to make her lovers
very distant.

'Well, you travel all over the country in
that trap, and you carry your wares underneath it, and you have no troubles, no cares,
no anxieties; how I envy you. Heigh ho!
if we could but change places.'

Cheap Jack raised his eyes for a moment
and looked at her with something of a flash;
then he said with some bitterness,—

'My life is hard enough at times—not
one for such as you to envy. When
times is bad, its bad fare as the liges of
us gets, and when they're good 'taint every
public as is open to receive us. Some
folk's money isn't as good as others in this
world.'

'Oh, how delightful! that's just what is so
charming—uncertainty. I've often thought
I should like to live in a gipsy's covered
cart and go about the country.'

'When you do, may I be servant and put you up to the tricks of the trade.'

'Agreed.' And Violet laughed merrily as she sat swinging herself backwards and forwards on the old tree, delighting in the storm she saw full well she was awaking in this man's breast.'

'I suppose you know most of the people about here?' she asked after a short pause.

'Gentle and simple, my lady, for the most part. But where's the neighbourhood that Jack Varley don't know the folk. More about their histories too sometimes than they know themselves.'

'I daresay, I daresay. In which case it is better to be your friend than your foe,' and Violet laughed a little nervously.

'It ain't much as I says,' he answered. 'I'm a man of few words 'cept when I'm forced perfessionally to puff my wares. If I talked more I shouldn't hear so much.'

'It is quite wonderful how you make up all those beautiful speeches about your goods. I heard you once in Hurton market-place,' said Violet flatteringly.

'Don't I look like it?' and he dropped his voice almost to a whisper as he spoke. 'Me? Lor' bless ye, lady, I couldn't do it. It's a blind man as lives in a court out of St Paul's Churchyard in London as composes they puffs. It's a trade as well as another. I gets 'em into my head while I am having my solitary dinner or driving along the roads in my shay.'

'I'll write you one,' cried Violet, 'such a puff; it will bring you in pounds. Oh! what fun; and in return—'

'Whatever I can do for your ladyship for all your favours, your ladyship is to command,' and Mr Varley took to shuffling his feet once more, as though this new mark of Violet's esteem was quite too much for his nervous susceptibilities.

'Well, in return you shall do whatever I bid you—always.'

He took off his velvet cap and bowed, thus tacitly declaring his determination to do her bidding.

It was a strange compact, and one from which most women in Mrs Tremayne's position would have flinched; but to Violet a love of excitement and out-of-the-way adventure was so strangely mixed up with a strong desire to keep her place in society, that she looked upon the whole thing as a rare joke. Balloon travelling had evidently not given her a sufficient warning; since she was once more at Montarlis she imagined she had got over that little difficulty, notwithstanding Mr Sivewright's inuendoes.

Could she not utilise this man perhaps to pay off some of the grudges she owed the duchess's reverend friend? Ay, there was a question involving immense issues she thought, as she got up from her rather

uncomfortable seat and held out her hand
to the astonished Cheap Jack, who merely
touched it with the tips of his fingers, so
unaccustomed was he to have anything so
fair and dainty presented to him.

'I must go now, but I'll see you again
here next Monday. We shall be going to
London soon ; there is a marriage and some
festivities in prospect, to which all the Montarlis party is going.'

And so they parted, Cheap Jack going
rather thoughtfully in the direction of his
little cart, Mrs Tremayne tripping through
the wood singing the refrain of a light
French song, and looking as pleased over
her anomalous *rencontre* as though her new
admirer were a prince in disguise.

The sound of a gun being fired off close
to her made her start.

'What ! shooting this covert. I thought
you were miles away,' she said as several
men, the duke and George Desborough

among them, came plunging through some
brushwood and stood before her.

'It is lucky you did not have an eye put
out or your hand shot off,' said the duke.
'Whoever expected to meet you here?'

'I never wish anybody to know where
they may expect to meet me,' she answered
laughing. 'Life is far too short to be
arranged by rule and rote. How do you do,
Mr Desborough? When last we met 'twas
in a balloon.'

George coloured up—her cool effrontery
somewhat abashed him; and the duke
scowled and went on—the mention of that
episode invariably made him angry—it was
entirely out of drawing; that is, as the picture of human life should be sketched
according to his views.

'It is not my fault that we have not met,'
George whispered as the duke walked away.
'Why do you so cruelly forbid me all sight
of you?'

' Perhaps an account of that hydra-headed termagant—gossip—perhaps, because the less you see of me the more you will pine for my society.'

'Oh, Mrs Tremayne, how cold and untrue.'

' Untrue ! Oh no, believe me, Mr Desborough, I know your sex better than you do yourself, though you are one of them.'

' Only tell me that you care for me just a little, and I will patiently attend your bidding and wait the probationary time.'

' Care for you ; it will take me all that time to read my heart—six months, was it not ? I am not so quick at mastering a subject as you are.'

' Ah, Violet—Violet, you are seeking to deceive yourself and me. If you do not love me, why are you here now ? '

' Not to meet you—on my oath—though I like you all the better for suggesting it ;

most men in your position would conceitedly
have thought that I wandered this way on
the chance of an interview, while you have
been honest enough to charge me with it.   I
will be equally plain-spoken with you—I
came on a totally different errand.'

'To meet some one else ?'

'Perhaps—' she laughed gaily ; 'but see,
the duke and the others have gone on—they
are nearly out of sight ; you seem absolutely
bent on compromising me.'

And before he had time to utter another
word she ran off, trilling once more the
refrain of the old French song, and leaving
him with that pregnant word 'perhaps'
rankling in his mind

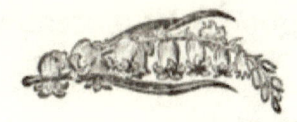

CHAPTER XV.

'DOTES YET DOUBTS.'

PRETTY Claire is lying on the sofa in her mother's room at Swanover Cottage. She is watching the fitful flames as they come and go in a wood fire, which has been lighted for her especial benefit — more as a companion than on account of chilliness ; but from the circlets round her eyes it is obvious that her thoughts scarcely go with her glance, but are dwelling on some dismal subject in connection with her own trials in life. Matthew has gone ! A presentiment of evil came to Claire with the knowledge that he was to be sent away, but the last fare-wells have been said. He regards the parting only as a brief cessation of their daily walks; not as a broken cord, but as an elastic band which stretched at will returns forthwith to its former limit. Alas! how often do not even elastic bands increase in size by stretching, and sometimes snap at a fragile touch. To Claire, for some indefinable reason which she could not have explained, even to her mother, it seemed as though the cord-elastic—call it what you will—had already snapped. She had seen Matthew come and go during his many Oxford vacations, and had fed her pets as usual, visited her poor as she was wont— now, she lay passively there and cared to take interest in naught. True, she had not loved Matthew in those days, or rather she had not owned her love; but did it not lie hidden in her heart, however much she might seek to ignore its presence?

Matthew had gone, to come back no more. Oh, bodily in the flesh, he would

be instinct with life, she had no apprehension
of his speedy dissolution ; but that he would
be hers—her very own to care for and to
caress she doubted. Some phantom—some
grim shadowy phantom—seemed to stand
before her, as though presiding over the
destinies of the man she loved. Lady
Laura said but little—what could she say ?
She shared all too fully her daughter's views,
and dreaded even more than she did the
influence which she felt sure would be
brought to bear on Matthew in London.

She was sitting reading, or pretending to
read, in the window, while Claire with
swollen eyes and aching brow was contem-
plating the flaming fuel. At last the girl
jumped up with a sudden energy.

' Mamma, this is wrong and wicked.
Matthew would be quite angry if he saw
me so dispirited ; let us go out.'

The maternal book was closed on the
instant.

'Yes, my love, the air will, I am sure, do you good. Why you are so down-hearted I can't think' (in her heart she knew full well). 'Matthew has only gone away for a little while.'

'He has gone for ever. Some one may come back, but it will not be Matthew; and what is a shell without the kernel?'

'These are mere superstitious fancies, child; what has he said to make you imagine these things?'

'Nothing, mother; but don't you think that the people among whom Matthew has been sent will teach him more of philosophy than love, and that after he has been a few weeks in this new world which Mr Sivewright has discovered for him, I shall appear a poor little ignorant country mouse, possessing no power to attract or please him.'

'Claire, if you have so mean an opinion of Matthew Desborough's faith and self-reliance, how is it you love him, my child ?'

' Because the heart is wayward, I suppose, and will not be guided by the mind's conviction. I love Matthew because I love him, not altogether because I trust him. Ah me !'

' My daughter, my Claire, it is a fearful thing that you are saying ; you love without trust, without belief. It is the most dangerous rock against which a woman can dash her earthly happiness.'

' I know it mother—know it, oh, so well. Have I not fought against it, been scared by Matthew's addresses, prayed, wept when you knew nothing of my feelings ? But the love was strongest, and I had to yield. If I die of misery I can resist no more.'

' But why should you doubt him, Claire. He is good and kind and manly—above all, possessed of a strong religious faith. He is almost too much of an enthusiast in fact.'

'Ah, mother, his zeal is hot but his faith is weak. Matthew must have a code to which to trust for guidance and support. Pray God it may always be the true one.'

Lady Laura looked at Claire in some surprise; she had never before known that her little daughter possessed such analytical discrimination; true, Claire had always been a quiet thoughtful child, and perhaps from the very fact that she had habituated herself from infancy to think much and talk but little of her feelings, was she the more capable of shaping them into words, now that under the influence of a great excitement she felt the necessity of revealing her inmost thoughts to her mother.

> 'Give sorrow words ; the grief that does not speak,
> Whispers the o'er-fraught heart and bids it break.'

'What reason have you to think that Matthew will fall away from his faith, my Claire?'

'Because he wants strength of purpose,

mother, and is easily led by the opinions of those around him.'

'Yet he is clever,' murmured rather than said Lady Laura.

'Too clever, perhaps,' answered poor Claire dolefully; 'if he did not seek to know too much, he would be more satisfied with what he has already learned.'

'You love Matthew, yet you do not respect him. You regard him as weak and vacillating. Oh, Claire, it is a miserable picture; strange too that Mr Sivewright should form the same judgment.'

'Has he—'

But Lady Laura's question remained unasked. Claire's head was turned away, lying among the sofa cushions, and she was sobbing as though her heart would break.

'They will take him from me in London,' she cried. 'Mr Sivewright knows full well the effect absence will have on Matthew.'

'But Claire, listen to reason; you have

promised to be this man's wife ; he is pledged to you by every law of honour. If a few months' absence makes him break his word, how do you think it would stand a life test, my child ? Be brave, my little girl, true to yourself—true to your womanhood. If Matthew is unfaithful to his allegiance, call on your pride for armour. It is a woman's glorious panoply, my daughter, and woe be to her who allows it to be trampled under her feet ; for she loses both her self-respect and the respect of her fellows.'

Claire sat up while her mother was talking, and wiping the large drops from her eyes, looked at her almost vacantly, as though the weight of all this reasoning were too much for her aching heart and head.

' I will do my best,' she said after a short pause, ' and, mother, you will help me, will you not ?' Lady Laura's arms were round her, and the aching bewildered head was laid on the truest heart that would ever beat for Claire.

Yet Lady Laura felt she must be 'cruel only to be kind.' Nursing Claire's sick fancies was scarcely the way to cure them, so she bade her daughter bathe her face in fresh cold water, put on her hat and come out.

'We will go and see some of our poor pensioners,' she said; 'by witnessing their sufferings, perhaps we shall be enabled to forget our own. We will not talk of Matthew any more.'

The girl, accustomed to obey her mother's slightest wishes, complied at once. In the course of half-an-hour they were going the tour of the cottages, Lady Laura talking on every subject which she thought was likely to interest Claire; but it was almost hopeless, the girl's white face and pre-occupied look disheartened the mother, who already regretted the day when the thunder-storm had brought about that unexpected interview. Coming back through the little wood they met Mr Lently—Father Lently as he elected to be called by his parishioners. He lifted his large soft clerical wide-a-wake when he saw them, perhaps feeling as much as they did that it was an unfortunate meeting ; but considering the parochial relations which existed between them, there was no alternative but to stop.

Lady Laura had had no conversation with Mr Lently on the subject of Matthew Desborough, but she knew, partly by intuition and partly from hints Matthew himself had dropped, that some of the recent occurrences were in accordance with the vicar's views of seemliness and well-doing. Perhaps she scarcely wished to discuss the subject with him, and had consequently kept out of his way ; be it as it might, she held her hand out to him with all cordiality—a cordiality which was in no wise reciprocated in the vicar's manner. He merely touched her fingers lightly, as he said harshly,—

'I have just been to Swanover. I wish

to have a little conversation with you about our young friend Matthew Desborough, over whom it seems you have of late been gaining an undue amount of influence.'

'Some other time I shall be very happy,' answered Lady Laura stiffly, making an effort to save Claire from an unpleasant discussion.

'Some other time, Lady Laura; do you not know that by procrastination a living soul may be lost?'

'Full well do I know it,' she said warmly. 'Yet I scarcely realise that any conversation you and I may have about Matthew touches on so grave a subject.'

'Have you not been instrumental in sending him to London, in order that, away from my teaching, he may be more amenable to your views?'

'The question is so injurious as to be almost insulting,' and Lady Laura reddened, as she drew herself up proudly.

He seemed somewhat astonished ; in the character of the good, benevolent, amiable Lady Laura, he had forgotten to look for the substratum of pride which she, however, knew full well how to lay bare at will. Before he had time to make any remark, she went on,—

'You will kindly allow me to postpone the discussion of this subject ; fix any hour you like, and I will grant you an interview.'

Lady Laura dictating terms and time to that arch-autocrat, the Vicar of Ravensholme, was so utterly paradoxical that, strange to say, from its very novelty, it was blandly received.

'To-morrow after matins,' he said, as he once more lifted his soft hat.

Lady Laura bowed and passed on, followed by Claire, who looked utterly bewildered.

Mr Lently had never even looked at her, and to find herself thoroughly ignored by her pastor was another drop of bitterness added to the cup, which was filling all too completely for poor Claire's powers of endurance.

' Mamma, what does it mean ? Have I done anything wicked ? ' she asked as soon as Mr Lently was out of hearing.

' You ?—no, my child. It means that you and Matthew are being made the victims of the dissensions which are rending our poor dear English Church. Rival opinions are fighting for Matthew—poor Matthew ! May he have strength to bear the brunt of the conflict ! '

' Oh, mamma ! how very dreadful it all is ! What can I do ? '

' Nothing, Claire, but pray and be patient ; be true to your faith and to yourself, and if, as God grant may not prove the case, you have drawn a blank in the great lottery of life, remember you will not be the first woman who has suffered for her love's sake.'

END OF VOL I.

COLSTON AND SON, PRINTERS, EDINBURGH.

www.ingramcontent.com/pod-product-compliance
Lightning Source LLC
Chambersburg PA
CBHW030808020726
47499CB00006B/1826